Stella Bonasera shook  and started to take p of rubble that was on building. She was about to suggest that Hawkes examine the bodies, but when she looked over her shoulder she saw that he was already squatting next to the body of Henry Doohan.

Sheldon Hawkes, kit on the ground beside him, leaned over the corpse, wiped rain from his eyes and looked at Doohan's bruised and dirty face. He turned the body on its side.

Stella had just taken her last photograph when she heard Hawkes call out, "This one was shot."

She put the camera away and was about to step toward the kneeling Hawkes when he said, "I think I hear something."

He pointed down a few feet from Doohan's body.

Stella backhanded rain from her face and looked in the direction Hawkes indicated. It was time to change gloves, but it wouldn't be easy taking off and putting on wet ones.

A sound. A crack. A deep breath from the earth.

Stella looked toward Hawkes to see if he had heard the sound, too. But Sheldon Hawkes had disappeared.

CSI:NY™

DELUGE

a novel

Stuart M. Kaminsky

Based on the hit CBS series "CSI: NY"
Produced by CBS Productions, a Business Unit of
CBS Broadcasting Inc. and
Alliance Atlantis Productions Inc.
Executive Producers: Jerry Bruckheimer,
Anthony E. Zuiker, Ann Donahue, Carol Mendelsohn,
Andrew Lipsitz, Danny Cannon, Pam Veasey,
Jonathan Littman
Series created by: Anthony E. Zuiker,
Ann Donahue, Carol Mendelsohn

POCKET STAR BOOKS
New York   London   Toronto   Sydney

An *Original* Publication of POCKET BOOKS

A Pocket Star Book published by
POCKET BOOKS, a division of Simon & Schuster, Inc.
1230 Avenue of the Americas, New York, NY 10020

This book is a work of fiction. Names, characters, places and incidents are products of the author's imagination or are used fictitiously. Any resemblance to actual events or locales or persons, living or dead, is entirely coincidental.

ISBN-13: 978-1-4165-1342-1
ISBN-10:   1-4165-1342-6

First Pocket Star Books paperback edition June 2007

10 9 8 7 6 5 4 3 2 1

POCKET STAR BOOKS and colophon are registered trademarks of Simon & Schuster, Inc.

Cover design by Richard Yoo
Photo of street © Jae Song

Manufactured in the United States of America

For information regarding special discounts for bulk purchases, please contact Simon & Schuster Special Sales at 1-800-456-6798 or business@simonandschuster.com.

Thanks to Lee Lofland
for his continuing help and his expertise.

CSI:NY™
DELUGE

1

SEVEN INCHES OF RAIN had fallen in Central Park. Worms inched out of warm mud in a doomed search for dry ground. Homeless men and women had long since gathered whatever possessions they had in makeshift bundles and made their way out of the park in soggy shoes and sneakers.

One of the homeless, a woman named Florence who was prone to delusions, wandered off the no-longer-discernable path and into the lake where she drowned, clutching a photograph of two dogs.

Signs were posted for people to stay out of the park, though the park seemed no more a victim of the deluge than the rest of the island of Manhattan.

But it would be all right, everything would be under control, if the weather got no worse. But it did get worse. Much worse.

• • •

The hard-driving September rain slapped against
Dexter Hughes's rain poncho as he stepped over
the river that rushed wildly next to the curb on
the north side of Eighty-seventh Street. Thunder
crashed in the 9 a.m. morning dimness. It was
music; loud, drums, brass. Music.

He paused to catch his breath and to make sure
his St. Paul medal was still around his neck and
that none of his wares had escaped from the bulg-
ing plastic Bloomingdale's bags he held.

Nothing was lost. Dexter smiled. Yes, it was his
kind of day. The radio had said it would probably
be the heaviest rain the city had experienced in
more than a century. Eight inches, maybe more,
today alone.

The malodorous water rushed along the street
next to the curb in front of him. An empty plastic
pill bottle bobbed down the river. Dexter could
make out a blue disposable razor, a filthy work
glove, a discarded Metrocard, a mangled white
ballpoint pen and the inch-high upper torso of a
Betty Boop figurine.

Half a block away he could make out men and
women running, leaping, hunching over with
purses, newspapers and umbrellas over their
heads. It was going to be a good day.

He pushed open the door of the Brilliance Deli
and stepped inside. The narrow aisle leading to

the six tables in the rear was thick with people exuding heavy, musty dampness, jammed together waiting for a break in the rain, a break that wasn't coming. They drank coffee, ate muffins and bagels and donuts, made calls on their cell phones, lost their tempers. Waited.

Dexter looked at Achmed, the deli's owner, who paused in his rush from grill to cash register. Dexter caught his eye and Achmed nodded his approval.

Dexter called out, "Umbrellas five dollars, rain ponchos three dollars."

He had picked up three dozen umbrellas and the same number of ponchos from Alvino Lopez at a graffitti-covered garage on 101st Street. He would have charged a dollar more if the merchandise did not carry the distinctive smell of motor oil.

Arms stretched out, eager for his wares. Dexter served out rain gear to cash-filled hands.

Rain beat down on the awning in front of the Brilliance. So did runoff water from the roof of the three-story brick building. A hole in the awning looked like an open faucet.

The sight was a godsend for Dexter, a sign to those huddled inside the deli that they needed protection.

Under his poncho, Dexter was a stick figure, as black and narrow as one of his umbrellas. Once, not all that many years ago, Dexter Hughes had commanded combat companies in battle in two wars. In the second of those wars, a small steel ball, one of hundreds released from a single bomb, had screeched through the night and torn out his right eye, taking part of the socket with it. Friendly fire tragedy. The army had fitted him with a state-of-the-art eye that looked natural enough if his good eye happened to be facing the same direction as the artificial one.

"Umbrellas imported from the South American rain forests, five dollars," Dexter called over the rain and voices. "Ponchos from Central America that defy rain, three dollars."

He shrugged inside his poncho to demonstrate how the water flew off. Customers nearby took a step back and then moved forward again. Ten- and twenty-dollar bills were held out.

"Umbrella." "Poncho." "Umbrella and a poncho, ten dollars. I need change, single dollar bills."

Hands were still reaching. Dexter shoved bills in his pockets. The Bloomingdale's bags grew lighter.

"That's it," said Dexter, giving out change for a twenty to a man who reeked of wet tobacco.

His bags empty, Dexter was considering a run back to the garage on 101st for more goods. Few wanted the rain to continue, but Dexter was one of the few.

"What the hell?" came a man's voice.

"Oh my God," said a woman.

"What is it?" said another woman. "What?"

They were looking over Dexter's shoulder. He turned and saw red rain gush through the tear in the awning.

Dexter could smell it. He had smelled it in two wars. Blood. He knew the look of blood in water, the dark, languid look.

The people in the deli and outside of it under the awning were talking. He sensed that Achmed had made his way through the crowd.

Dexter stepped out into the rain, avoiding the bloody stream. He looked up, blinking through the downpour.

Three stories above him, Dexter could see a man standing at the edge of the roof, something in his hand. The man was wearing a dark GI raincoat. The man's eyes met Dexter's. A torrent of blood and water poured from a drainage spout on the roof just beneath the man, who slowly straightened and turned. Then the man was gone.

Dexter wouldn't be going back to pick up more umbrellas and ponchos and he wouldn't be waiting around for the police. He had had more than enough encounters with the police, thank you.

Dexter turned and headed into the deluge, resisting the urge to look over his shoulder and up at the roof behind him.

Dexter knew the man on the roof and the man on the roof knew him.

• • •

The man limped away from the edge of the roof. The black man in the yellow poncho had met his gaze. They had recognized each other. Then the black man had moved away into the almost painful slam of thick, demanding rain.

A half century of stones on the roof mixed with the detritus of broken beer bottles, shriveled condoms, and discarded syringes that were carried away in the red river. The potted plants lined up against the knee-high walls were overflowing and adding black dirt and chemicals to the rushing water.

The flat rooftop had a simple drainage system that allowed rainwater to run off to prevent ponding, which would damage the roof covering. Around the outside edge of the rooftop were low places that served as funnels. The funnels or scuppers emptied into holes in the parapet wall toward both the street and alley. Inside these scuppers were rusting screens to catch debris. From time to time, particularly after a hard rain, someone would clear away the debris from the screen. The woman that the man had just killed had been on the roof to clear those screens.

The man was transfixed, nearly hypnotized, knowing he should move, get away. He had a lot left to do and very little time. Instead he stared down at the dead woman.

She was spread-eagled, dress hiked up, skin exposed. There was a look of horror on her face, horror and pain. Her hair was beaten back, clamped to her head. She looked almost bald. Her open mouth was filled with water that bubbled as if from an overfilled pool.

The man hadn't known what he would feel when he killed her. He'd hoped that he wouldn't regret it, wouldn't be haunted, wouldn't shake or weep. He wanted to savor the moment. He wanted elation, satisfaction, not this dull, dreamy sensation echoing to the beat of thoughtless, demanding rain.

He lifted his head and closed his eyes. Rain pelted his face. He drank, gulped with thirst, broke the spell, folded the knife and pocketed it.

He took one last look at the mutilated body sprawled on the stones of the roof. It was time to go. He was satisfied.

He limped toward the door.

About half the students of Wallen School on West End Avenue had not shown up for classes that morning. All the teachers had made their way, some coming from Brooklyn, Queens, the Bronx, places where they could afford the rent on teachers' salaries and still have something left over so they could eat.

Wallen, grades K through 12, had a strict policy and exclusive criteria for admission. If you could afford the tuition, which was twenty-seven thousand a year, you were in.

Wayne O'Shea, thirty-four, who the students called Brody behind his back because of his faint resemblance to the actor Adrien Brody, was one of those who made the daily pilgrimage from Brooklyn. He had been doing it for the past six years, long enough for his salary to climb up to a living wage. Wayne was gay, which was not a drawback at Wallen, where the faculty included two blacks, three Hispanics, one gay man, and a bearded Muslim who were proudly displayed for prospective parents.

First period, English Literature II, had gone as he had expected. Only seven students, the ones who lived within fifteen minutes of the school, sat in a gray state of dream unable to resist the sight of the torrent, easily able to resist D. H. Lawrence. Wayne couldn't blame them. He himself had gone from avid champion of Lawrence when he was in college to bored adult when *Lady Chatterly's Lover* came around on the reading list.

Five minutes before class ended, Gayle Swoops, whose father was a famous rapper, was lazily trying to come up with an answer to the question Wayne had posed. It should have been easy. Wayne had no specific answer in mind.

There was a thud and crash in Alvin Havel's chemistry lab next door. Nothing unusual. From time to time, students, especially those coming in in the morning still high from some new designer drug, were known to drop some fragile things and knock over other not-so-fragile things.

Neither Gayle nor any of the other students, drummed into oblivion by rain and Lawrence, had noticed.

"Give it a try," Wayne said in an attempt to rescue Gayle Swoops. "As Lawrence once said, 'When one jumps over the edge, one is bound to land somewhere.'"

Through the speakers in the hall outside the classrooms and throughout Wallen, the gentle two notes of a mallet against a hollow wooden box announced the end of class. The students slowly rose. A few smiled at Wayne. They all had a long day ahead of them.

Ten minutes between classes. Wayne, casual, hands in pockets, ambled into the uncrowded hall, the voices and footsteps of the students muted by polished oak floors and thick. dark-stained wooden walls.

The chemistry lab door was closed. It was common for either Wayne or Alvin to seek each other out between classes to exchange a few words of support or a witty and not always kind observation about one of the kids or one of the other teachers.

Alvin was straight, thirty-seven, married, two daughters, and a wife who made more money than he did. Alvin had been working forever at night to finish his PhD and find a college-level job, preferably in New York, but anywhere but Wallen Prep would do. If it happened, Wayne would miss him. When he opened the door to the chemistry lab, Wayne was certain it would never happen.

Alvin was seated, head turned on the steel-topped desk facing Wayne. Alvin wore a mask of blood. A pencil jutted out of his left eye. Another pencil was plunged into his neck.

Wayne stood there for a few seconds, registering what he saw before him. He swayed, felt dizzy.

"Little fucking bastards," Wayne, who never cursed, said, and took a step toward the desk. The door behind him opened. Voices.

Wayne started to turn, felt acrid bile rise in his throat.

Then he passed out.

Malcom Cheswith had ambition. He someday wanted to be a renowned Cajun and Creole chef, but for now he was a short-order cook. Malcom could be patient. Things would take a turn for the better soon.

In the meantime, whenever possible, Malcom made magic in the small space that passed for a kitchen in Doohan's Bar on Catherine Street. Malcom could barely turn around in the kitchen, even though he was weasel thin from the years of drenching kitchen heat and the gift of his mother's genes.

There was no real reason for him to be there this early in the morning with the rain coming down in thick, dark curtains. The few morning regulars there were not eaters. Doohan was the morning bartender. Doohan was also the owner of Doohan's, but whatever he could pull in without paying a barkeep was more money for the mortgage, which Doohan had been having trouble meeting. Malcom was on half salary for the morning, a grudging concession by Doohan, who didn't want to lose his short-order cook.

One reason the very fat Doohan didn't want to lose his cook was that Doohan appreciated fine cooking and was a willing consumer and critic when Malcom decided to prepare something special. This morning Malcom was preparing Eggs Sardou; poached eggs and creamed spinach on artichoke bottoms with hollandaise sauce. Malcom was practicing his culinary skill and Doohan would normally be practicing his gluttony. Today, however, he had no appetite.

There were three customers in the dark bar, which smelled more than faintly of beer and where music was never played. Later, more customers, mostly cops who were working out of the courthouse a few blocks away on Worth Street, would join the blue-collar retirees, who, like Doohan, were comfortable with the smell and the silence.

Thunder rattled the window where the neon Miller Lite Beer sign flickered for an instant. The bar went dark. One of the regulars, Frank Zvitch, did not flinch. He adjusted his railroad engineer's cap, waited, and when it was clear the lightning had stopped and the lights would stay on at least for a while, he resumed the story he was telling and nursed his beer.

Today Frank talked to Anthony DeLuca, who stood no more than five foot two and wore flannel shirts and suspenders to remind people that he had been a longshoreman. Over the years, Anthony had told his stories so often that he couldn't be sure if they had happened to him or if he had picked them up by watching Pop Doyle too many times in *On the Waterfront*. Whenever possible, Anthony demonstrated his permanent slouch and the fact that one arm, his right, was shorter than his other. Unlike Frank, Anthony kept the frosty mugs of frothy beer coming. He held his drink well, never got drunk, not even close.

Malcom looked up from time to time as he cooked, wiped his brow and consumed glass after glass of cold tap water that today tasted a bit suspicious. Doohan was standing by the window, his back to Malcom, looking out even though it was nearly impossible to see through the thick sheets of rain.

The sauce was almost ready. Malcom, born in Chicago, had been lured by the kitchens of New Orleans and tales of a brother who had acted in theaters in Dublin, Canberra, London, Toronto and the American South. But Malcom had been pulled by necessity and a now dead, sick sister to Manhattan. Hopefully he could leave one day. Malcom's Eggs Sardou could be a step in the right direction.

When Malcom looked up again, Frank and Anthony were listening to each other and Doohan was stepping out the door into the rain.

Through the steamy window flowing with rivulets, he could make out the almost cartoon outline of Doohan. He was wearing no raincoat. Next to him was another shape, a man, taller than the bar owner, erect, about Malcom's height, wearing a raincoat and hood. Were they arguing? The taller man started to move away, but Doohan grabbed his arm, or it looked to Malcom as if he were grabbing the tall man's arm. It looked like a struggle. Doohan looked at the window. His eyes would have met Malcom's had Doohan been focused beyond the window.

Lightning. The tall man's face hidden by the hood; Doohan's face open, white, panicked. The few hairs on his head plastered to his scalp, a Zero Mostel imitation.

The tall man took another step away into the

torrent. Doohan again pulled at the tall man's sleeve. The tall man tried to get away but he slipped on the sidewalk. Both men tripped through the front door of the bar, Doohan still holding on to the sleeve of the tall man. What Malcom and the regulars at the bar saw next was incredible, unbelievable and also the last thing they ever saw.

The world ended.

The explosion came from Malcom's right. The wall began to crumble and squeal. Frank and Anthony just managed to get off their bar stools as the ceiling groaned and began to fall slowly like an elevator in slow motion. There was a second explosion and Malcom was thrown back against the grill. He put a hand behind him to steady himself as the building screeched. His hand rested on the searing grill. He smelled burning flesh but knew that he had a far bigger problem than a scorched palm.

Pots, pans toppled. Sauce spilled. Artichokes flew. Malcom tried to remain standing, tried to make his way to the narrow kitchen door without falling. He failed.

The building was imploding. He could no longer see Frank or Anthony nor the bar or the window or Doohan or the tall man. Malcom went down when the refrigerator rose toward him and the floor came up at a rollercoaster angle.

Then there was an instant of silence.

Then there was a settling groan of walls, ceiling, tilted furniture and a section of the bar falling with a delayed thud.

Then there was a voice.

Then there was the rain.

2

IT WAS THE SIXTH DAY of rain. Ten people had been reported electrocuted by fallen power lines. Flooding in some subway lines had stopped trains. An Indonesian cab driver driven mad by the inching traffic on Second Avenue shot a Jamaican cabbie who had stalled out in front of him. Trash cans and dumpsters were turned over and garbage cascaded down streets. Rats scurried up from the sewers, running for the nearest building.

"Alf the sacred river is running amok," shouted one of Manhattan's army of mad street corner and subway prophets. He was a gangly creature with obligatory scraggly beard. He called out calmly, loudly over the beat, beat, beat of the rain. He would have been completely ignored if it weren't for the fact that he was completely nude. As it was, almost everyone passing by either ignored him or pretended to.

New Yorkers had seen it all. Well, almost all. There was still plenty to behold.

Under the crime scene tent on the rooftop above the Brilliance Deli, Detective Mac Taylor snapped photographs of the mutilated corpse, the few faint traces of blood that hadn't been washed away, the potted plants along the walls, the runoff holes and funnels. The dead woman whose skirt was pushed up was about fifty years old, slightly heavy-set, short dark hair with visible graying at the roots.

Mac had already taken dozens of photographs of the roof before he even entered the tent.

At Mac's side, Officer George Weathers, young, stone faced, shrouded in his dark raincoat, looked at Mac. Weathers had seen enough of the corpse.

"Call came at two minutes after nine," said Weathers over the beating sound of the rain on the tent. "Deli owner downstairs. Said blood was pouring on his awning. I got here just before ten. I was over on Lex helping an old man with a heart attack."

Weathers was talking to avoid looking at the corpse, thinking about it, being haunted by it. Mac understood. "Who is she?" he asked.

"Patricia Mycrant, resident in this building,

apartment sixteen. Lives . . . lived with her mother, Gladys Mycrant."

Mac nodded again. The scene had been badly compromised by rain and the delay in his getting here. It had taken him and Detective Donald Flack forty minutes. Normally, it would have taken ten minutes from the forensics lab. If it hadn't been for Flack's stock car driving, it would have taken at least twenty minutes longer.

Water dribbled down Mac's neck under his raincoat. He ignored it.

"Search the roof for a weapon. Then search the ground on all sides of the building. After that, the hallways and the rooftop next door. Talk to the deli owner, anyone else, customers, waiters, cooks," said Mac. "Ask if they saw anyone going into the building before nine or coming out after they saw the bloody rain."

He and Flack would go over the rooftops and hallways and check on every tenant in the building. It didn't hurt to keep Weathers busy and he might turn something up.

"Right," said Weathers, who quickly left the tent.

Mac knelt next to the dead woman, took a dozen more photographs and then placed the waterproof camera in his kit. Then he examined the corpse of Patricia Mycrant.

There was a blood-tinged slit next to her left breast, just under her arm. Mac carefully unbuttoned her rain-drenched shirt and examined the neat wound. With latex gloves on his hands he gently touched the flesh around the wound. No ribs were broken. Whoever struck this blow either knew what he or she was doing or got very lucky.

It was very possible, even likely, given the look on the dead woman's face, that she had been alive while the mutilation occurred.

Mac removed small glass vials from his kit a few feet away and took samples from the wounds. Mac didn't use plastic containers. The possibility of the plastic contaminating a sample was a chance he was unwilling to take. His team had been stung at trial once because of possible contamination of evidence in a plastic vial. It wouldn't happen again.

The body would have to be taken to the lab where an autopsy would determine how many times the woman had been stabbed, how deep the wounds had been. If they were lucky and thorough, the autopsy would also provide some information about the weapon including its length, thickness, width and, if the weapon chipped off or hit bone or hard tissue, there might be enough evidence to identify the knife if it was found. If the weapon was found in the possession of the killer, residue—blood, shards of metal—could also identify it as the murder weapon.

The attack appeared to be sexual, but that could be a cover-up. An examination would determine if there had been penetration. If there had, there might be semen, which meant there might be DNA.

He moved the body slightly to check lividity and determined from the dark layer on the corpse's back that the woman had probably died where she lay. Beneath the body was a crumpled Starbucks coffee cup.

Mac took a photograph of the cup, then carefully deposited the cup in an evidence bag. Mac checked the dead woman's hands, scraped under her fingernails and deposited the residue in a tube.

After bagging her hands, Mac examined the pebbled rooftop around the body. He used a compact Alternate Light Source to look at and around the body again. The ALS was made up of a powerful lamp containing the ultraviolet visible and infrared components of light. The unit then filtered down the light into individual color bands or wavelengths that enhanced the visibility of evidence by the glow or fluorescence of evidence, the darkness of the evidence and small particles revealed by the light.

Although invisible to the naked eye, the ALS revealed a faint trail of blood that led beyond the tent. Mac followed the trail. It led him to the edge of the roof and to one of the drain funnels, the one through which the torrent of blood and rain had cascaded down to the awning below. Without touching the tile rim, Mac examined it. In the oily dirt there was a handprint the rain had not washed away.

Mac thought he could make out the hint of blood in the print. A scan of the print proved him right. There were no visible ridges in the print. The killer had probably worn gloves very much like the ones Mac was wearing. The prints would yield nothing, but the fact that the killer had stood at the edge of the roof might. Someone could have looked up, seen the killer. Not an outlandish possibility. Blood had cascaded down to the awning below. People had seen it. Someone might reasonably be curious enough to step out in the street and look up to see the killer with blood on his hands looking down.

Flack sat patiently, sympathetically across from Gladys Mycrant in her apartment. He had taken off his raincoat. She had hung it on a hanger in the bathroom after shaking it out.

He had his notebook and a pen in his lap. Until recently, members of the New York Police Department took notes in pencil. Pencil notes could be erased, altered. The district attorney's office did not like pencil notes.

Flack felt himself wince. Two, three, five times a day a shock of pain shot through him and he had to resist putting his hand to his chest to reassure himself that he wasn't bleeding, that his heart wasn't exposed and beating madly.

He had pills in his pocket, pills for the pain. He took them as seldom as possible. They dulled not only the pain but his senses.

Mac had saved his life in the rubble of a bombed-out office building in which they had been trapped. Flack had come very close to death. Sometimes he felt that life had not fully returned.

Gladys offered coffee. He had accepted both because he could use a cup of coffee and because it created a slightly less clinical atmosphere. The coffee was instant, not very hot, served in delicate, ornate, too small china cups. Flack usually took his coffee black. This time he took it with milk and sugar.

"She got a phone call, Patricia did," she said.

Gladys was sixty-eight, thin, wearing a robe that might have been authentic Chinese silk. Her hair was pulled back and her face made up. She was a professionally handsome woman. She was also remarkably calm for someone who had just been informed that her daughter had been murdered on the roof.

"Who called?" Flack asked.

"Don't know," she said, starting to lift her cup of coffee and changing her mind.

"The call came on that phone?" Flack asked, looking at the phone on the table between them.

"Yes."

"What did she say when she got the call?"

"She said she'd be right back, but she was wrong, wasn't she?"

"Yes," said Flack.

"She knew it was raining but she went out without an umbrella. She looked angry and frightened and in a hurry."

"You have any idea of who might want to hurt her?"

Gladys Mycrant smiled and shook her head.

"I can't think of a single person who would want to hurt Patricia."

"Anyone she's had an argument with? Boyfriend?"

"No boyfriend," said Gladys. "Not Patricia."

"Who were her friends?"

"None."

"None?"

"She was a lonely, bitter woman," said Gladys.

"Bitter?"

"Unlucky in love many years ago, more than once."

"Any names?"

"Lost in antiquity, Detective. Another lifetime. A decade ago."

Flack forced himself to drink some coffee. Maybe he and Mac could pick up a real cup in the deli downstairs.

"Did she have a job?"

"My daughter managed this building and the one right next door."

"Who owns the buildings?"

"I do. I should have offered you some Rugers. I'm fond of them but I ration my allotment. The carbs."

"Yes," said Flack.

"I own the buildings but I also work," she said. "Sales at Found Again on Ninth Avenue, the charity resale shop. We deal only in donated items from celebrities. People vie to give their clothes and costume jewelry to us, and customers love the idea of wearing a skirt that was recently worn by Britney Spears or a pair of Antonio Banderas's discarded shoes."

"Sounds interesting," said Flack.

"Fascinating," said Gladys with a sad smile. "This gown I'm wearing belonged to Cher."

"You don't seem . . . ?"

"Devastated by the gruesome murder of my daughter? We all suffer in different ways. I've learned to suffer in increments, not explosions, to expect disappointment. I'll grieve in my own way and not the way the world expects me to. Does that answer your question?"

"It does," said Flack. "Anything else you can think of that might help?"

"No, but I'm sure you will give me a card with

your name and phone number on it should something come to me."

"I will," he said. "May I look at your daughter's room?"

"You may not," she said.

He put away his notebook. "You have some reason?"

"I need none. My daughter just died. I dislike the image of you rustling around through her underclothes, her privacy."

"I can get a search warrant," he said gently. "This is a murder investigation."

"I'm sure you can and will, but on this issue you will not have my cooperation."

"There may be something in her room that can lead us to whoever killed her," Flack pressed. "The faster we move, the more likely we are to find him."

"Or her," Gladys Mycrant added. "Your plea would suggest that I have a vested interest in finding out who murdered my daughter. I have none. She is dead and not returning. Punishing the guilty party strikes me as irrelevant. It is your concern and business, not mine."

Flack knew that by the time he got a warrant, Gladys would be able to hide or dispose of anything in her daughter's room or the apartment that she didn't want the police to see. It wouldn't necessarily have anything to do with the murder, but it might.

"If the rain lets up, I'll be going to work this afternoon," she said, rising from her seat along with Flack. "It will take my mind off of what has happened. Good-bye, Detective."

"I'm very sorry for your loss," he said, moving to the door.

"Why?" she asked. "You barely know me and you did not know Patricia."

"I'm sorry for anyone who loses a child," he said.

"Patricia was forty-six years old, hardly a child."

Flack gave up. He had been doing interviews of suspects, victims and their families for more than ten years. He had met crazies who would confess to anything, killers who were sure they could get around the evidence, religious fanatics who didn't know the difference between real and unreal, but he had never met anyone like Gladys Mycrant. All he could be sure of about her was that she was both lying and hiding something. He wanted to find out what her secrets were. Those secrets might lead to a murderer.

Flack went to find Mac. Before calling to arrange for a search warrant, he was determined to have a real cup of coffee and maybe, just maybe, one of the pills in his pocket.

Earlier that morning, before his execution of Patricia Mycrant, the limping man paused in the hallway of an office building twenty-one blocks away. He had pulled the waterproof hood of his raincoat back so he could drink the tall Starbucks coffee he had purchased minutes before. The latex gloves made it slightly awkward, but only slightly.

The rain, deep, dark, protective, beat noisily, a dull tom-tom beat, a million drums, relentlessly uncaring, which was just what he wanted, why he had chosen this day, why he now stood in the hallway outside of Strutts, McClean & Berg on the eighth floor of the Stanwick Oil Building.

The limping man hadn't needed to follow James Feldt. He knew where Feldt would be. He was certain that Feldt would not be stopped by the rain. He knew enough about the man to know that staying in his studio apartment alone for even one full day would be intolerable. The limping man had counted on it.

James Feldt had no friends. His relatives had little to do with him and what contact they had was by snail mail, never face-to-face. James Feldt was fifty-two, pink baby face; luxuriant, fine, short white hair neatly combed at all times. The limping man had never seen James Feldt when he wasn't wearing a suit, and Feldt seemed to have an endless supply of suits, or at least sartorial variations.

Feldt wore granny glasses and thought he looked like John Lennon, which he decidedly did not.

James Feldt was an auditor, a good one judging by the number of clients he had throughout Manhattan. All of his work came by way of referrals. Most of his income was spent on books he kept in shelves in his apartment. Hundreds of books. Classics, ancient, old and modern. The books were all purchased used so they would look as if he had read them. He had not. James Feldt spent his free time on the Internet, in therapy sessions and working. His solace, his meditation was in numbers, not words. He clung to his laptop like a novitiate might cling to his Bible.

The limping man knew him well.

He finished the coffee. James Feldt was alone in the office. Most of the offices in the building were closed because of the weather. In most cases, employees, partners and management had just assumed it would not be business as usual. And they were right. Power kept flicking on and off. Now it was dark inside and outside the door to Strutts, McClean & Berg.

Feldt did not pause. Glasses perched on the end of his nose, he played at the keys of his battery-powered laptop and kept working.

The desktop computer he had turned off sat silently. He would turn it back on when the power was restored or the backup building generator kicked in. He had plenty to do until that happened.

The limping man drained the last few drops of coffee from the cup, crushed the cup and stuffed it into one deep pocket of his raincoat. With his free hand, he reached into the other deep pocket and took out the knife, the knife he would later use to carve, abuse, punish and kill Patricia Mycrant on a roof twenty-one blocks away.

The glass outer door wasn't locked. James Feldt had seen no reason to lock it. It wouldn't have mattered much if he had. The man would simply have knocked and waited till the curious auditor had opened the door. But this was much better.

The man, knife now open in his pocket, went through the outer door and walked to the inside office door that James had left open. He walked silently, though James wouldn't have heard him in any case against the background of rain.

Clap of thunder. Perfect. Perfect. A horror movie. A lone victim in an isolated room, a mad or calculating killer. But the limping man was most assuredly not mad.

He stood in the office doorway, waiting. He was not in a hurry, at least not in a big hurry. He waited for James to look up or sense that he was there. It didn't take long.

When James Feldt looked up, fingers arched lightly over the keyboard like a piano virtuoso, he was startled but not instantly surprised.

When James Feldt recognized the man in the

doorway of the office, the man who was closing the door behind him, he was not frightened. He was puzzled.

"You working in the building?" he asked, looking down at his screen, typing in a few words, finishing his thought before looking up again.

The limping man shook his head.

James was completely confused now, wrenched from the numbers he had danced with seconds ago.

"Then what are you doing here?"

The limping man took out the knife and showed the blade to the man seated behind the desk. James adjusted his glasses so he could better see what the man was holding.

The lights came back on and James had a good look at the man's face, but it wasn't the face that suddenly frightened him as much as the clear vision of the knife and the latex glove gripping it.

James sighed deeply, turned off his laptop and closed the lid.

"Which one?" James asked.

The man with the knife understood.

"All of them."

James rose quickly and ran to the window. The limping man was ready. He cut him off. James Feldt would not cheat him by throwing himself out the window.

The limping man pushed Feldt with his free

hand and slid the blade under his arm just below the left armpit. Feldt let out a sound like the air leaving a flat tire. He sank to the floor in a sitting position, trying to reach the wound.

He couldn't reach it. Not in time. He looked up. The sensation was strange, as if he had expected this or something very like it for some time.

James Feldt closed his eyes and prayed that the end would come quickly, but somehow he knew that it wouldn't.

3

"SMELL THAT?" DANNY MESSER SAID as he and Lindsay Monroe walked through the front door of the Wallen School.

In front of them, down the corridor, a uniformed policewoman motioned to them and pointed to a room to her left.

"Smell what?" asked Lindsay.

"Old wood," said Danny, adjusting his glasses. "Schools like this want that old wood atmosphere. Look at the walls. This place is maybe forty years old. Smells like it's a hundred and fifty. I think they spray that smell in here every morning. It's worth a couple of grand more on the tuition bill."

They were almost to the uniformed officer. Their footsteps echoed on the dark stained floor.

Danny reached over and opened the door the

policewoman had indicated. Lindsay had her camera out. Both Danny and Lindsay were already gloved, ready and watching where they stepped.

They had driven, hubcap deep, from the lab. They considered taking the subway, but were told the trains weren't moving. Danny had done the driving. Neither Danny nor Lindsay had spoken to each other during the ride. Danny had talked to the other motorists, criticizing their slowdowns, critiquing their driving.

Lindsay was silent because she had gotten a call from her mother in Montana. Her mother was worried about her. Her mother was addicted to The Weather Channel. The call had not gone well.

Danny was not speaking, at least not to Lindsay, because he had been rained out of a date with Augusta Wallace for the last four days. He had been working on Augusta, a beautiful, slim, dark-haired detective, for months before she finally gave in, but the delays were clearly giving her second thoughts. He could tell by her few words, her passing smile in the halls.

Stepping into the murder scene, Danny Messer cursed the rain and turned his full attention to the dead man on the desk with the pencils protruding from his left eye and neck.

"We're still digging out bodies," the fireman said, leaning back against the red truck.

He wiped his face with the heavy gray glove on his hand and took off his helmet. His last name was Devlin. Stella could see that from the name on his raincoat.

Devlin was young, tall, handsome and weary. That was as clear as the name on his coat. Behind him lay what little remained of Doohan's. It wasn't much, a fragment of the bar, an edge now tilted to create a waterfall of seemingly endless rain. The leg of a chair stuck straight up as if someone had planted it in the rubble to mark the location of a buried body. A frying pan lay upside down on top of a torn scrap of checkered cloth. The cloth lay limp, beaten down by the rain and clinging to jagged bits of plaster and debris. At Stella Bonasera's feet was an unbroken and unopened bottle of Dewar's Scotch.

"Not too much of a fire," said Devlin. "Happened quickly. Place collapsed. We're getting a lot of that. Roofs mostly. The rain knocks it down. But in this case it wasn't the rain that knocked it down."

"What makes you think that?" said Sheldon Hawkes, standing at Stella's side.

"The end posts on the bearing walls," Devlin said, nodding toward where the walls had been. "Three of them collapsed at the same time and they didn't just collapse on their own. You can still smell the dynamite, that liquidy sweet smell."

"I know the smell," said Stella.

"Official report'll come from an arson investigator," Devlin said. "We can call in the dogs to track it, but I'm sure."

"The dead?" asked Hawkes.

"Left where we found them," said Devlin. "That's what you want, that's what you get."

"It's what we need," said Stella.

"I'll lead the way," said Devlin, pushing himself away from the truck. "We're shorthanded. Half of the crew is on another call. You'd think rain would keep fires from breaking out, not cause them."

They followed him, walking carefully over a fun-house floor of pieces, bits, chips and jagged metal. Devlin stopped and pointed to a tarp.

"Didn't know whether to leave them in the rain or cover them and maybe preserve evidence," said Devlin.

"It's a toss-up," said Stella.

She had thrown back the hood of her raincoat to give herself a better view of the scene and whatever bodies she might find. Her hair tumbled in front of her eyes. She ran her fingers through it to keep it back. She pulled a thick rubber band from her pocket and awkwardly, the arms of her raincoat swishing heavily together, tied her hair back. Devlin smiled in appreciation of Stella's high forehead and Grecian features. Stella was aware of the fireman's appreciation. This wasn't the time or place. Stella knew it. Devlin knew it. They also knew from their jobs that feeling guilty about small natural reactions wasn't worthwhile.

"We pulled ID on all four of the dead men. They all had wallets," said Devlin.

He took a notebook from an inner pocket and shielded it with his jacket to read the names.

"This one is Frank Zvitch," said Devlin. "One next to him is Anthony DeLuca."

Stella pulled back the nearby tarp to reveal the headless body of DeLuca.

"Back there"—Devlin pointed—"Malcom Cheswith. Looks like he was the cook."

Stella raised an eyebrow.

"He's wearing an apron, has a grease burn on his palm. We found him just outside the kitchen."

Stella nodded.

"There, where the front door used to be." Devlin pointed to a tarp covering an inflated shape. "Henry Doohan, owner. Papers in his pocket."

"He's carrying ownership papers in his pocket?" asked Stella.

"Ownership, licenses, insurance, inspection sheets," said Devlin.

"Odd," said Stella.

"Odd," Devlin agreed. "Why would he be carrying them?"

Stella wished she could tent all four dead men, but they only had one tent in the trunk, just a small one that could handle one body, not big enough to stand in.

"We'll take it from here, Lieutenant," she said, removing her camera from the kit she put down.

Devlin nodded and moved away, wiping his face with his gloved hand.

"One more thing," he said. "Again, we have to wait for an arson investigator and I may be wrong, but it looks to me like the charges went off before they were supposed to."

"Could be," Stella agreed. "Dry dynamite is relatively safe to handle, but when it gets wet, it's highly unstable and volatile. It doesn't take much to set it off."

"That's what I was thinking," Devlin said. "You're Greek, right?"

"Right."

"Thought so," he said with a smile and walked away.

She shook rain from her face and eyes and started to take pictures. She was about to suggest that Hawkes examine the bodies, but when she looked over her shoulder she saw that he was already squatting next to the body of Henry Doohan.

Hawkes, kit on the ground beside him, leaned over the corpse, wiped rain from his eyes and looked at Doohan's bruised and dirty face. He turned the body on its side. He was sure.

Stella had just taken her last photograph when she heard Hawkes call out, "This one was shot."

She put the camera away and was about to step toward the kneeling Hawkes when he said, "I think I hear something."

He pointed down a few feet from Doohan's body.

Stella backhanded rain from her face and looked in the direction Hawkes indicated. It was time to change gloves, but it wouldn't be easy taking off and putting on wet ones.

A sound. A crack. A deep breath from the earth.

Stella looked toward Hawkes to see if he had heard the sound. But Sheldon Hawkes had disappeared.

"What've we got, Montana?" Danny asked Lindsay after they had photographed the scene. "Make what's left of my morning interesting."

He looked toward the front of the room, where the dead teacher lay over his desk.

"Testing me again?" Lindsay asked, crossing her arms.

"Would I do that?" he asked with a grin.

"Whenever you can."

She smiled.

They were standing in the back of the chemistry lab against a whiteboard with a list of chemicals carefully written on it in black marker. Three slate-topped lab tables were lined up in front of them. On each tabletop were burners, retorts, test tubes and a built-in sink. The room smelled of sulfur and a blend of chemicals not unlike those in the crime scene lab. The difference was that the Wallen School lab looked out of date by a century. But that, both Danny and Lindsay could tell, was an affectation like the hallways. The equipment was new, clean, modern. The cabinets were stocked with hundreds of neatly labeled bottles and jars, and two computers with high-speed Internet connections sat on each lab table.

Beyond these tables lay Alvin Havel, chemistry teacher, soccer coach and winner of Teacher of the Year for the past four years according to the plaques placed tastefully on the wall next to the only door to the room.

"Someone strong or very angry or both," said Lindsay. "Both wounds. I'll get a package of pencils on the way back to the lab."

"Two packages," said Danny.

"Right," agreed Lindsay.

Two different kinds of red pencil had been plunged into Alvin Havel. One, a normal #2 into his eye, the other an extra thick #4 into his neck.

She didn't have to say more on this issue. She would take the pencils, get a dead pig from the refrigerator and determine exactly how much pressure it had taken to plunge the pencils in as deeply as they had gone. The body density of a pig was remarkably close to that of a human.

"What else?" Danny asked, arms folded.

"Wound to the neck was first. That's what killed him. He was standing. The blow is straight across. If he were sitting, it would be downward. To strike straight across while he was sitting would mean the killer would have to be on his—"

"Or her—"

"Knees or squatting. Not much leverage and judging by the depth of the pencil, the blow was hard."

"That it?" asked Danny, looking at the dead man.

"Blood splatter from the neck wound supports what I just said."

"And the pencil in the eye?"

"Not as deep," she said. "We've got a puzzle with that wound. He was already dead when the eye trauma happened. No blood splatter. No beating heart."

"Someone stabbed a dead man?" asked Danny.

"Maybe they didn't know he was dead?"

"Pencil plunged into his neck, eyes open. Hard to miss."

"Puzzle," Lindsay agreed. "Two different attackers?"

"Maybe."

"The killer had blood, lots of it, on him—"

"Or her."

"Security tapes," she said.

The security cameras in the Wallen School halls were not concealed, nor were they obvious. Their purpose was to let students know they were being watched at all times. Danny knew schools all over the city that had dummy cameras mounted on the walls. Real working ones were too expensive. Wallen School, however, would have the money to have working surveillance.

"None in this room," said Lindsay.

"Teachers don't like them in the classrooms," said Danny.

"Academic freedom," she said.

"Something like that. We look at the tape, but first we talk to the teacher who discovered the body and the students who were in the class when Havel was killed. Maybe we get lucky and get a Perry Mason."

A Perry Mason was a confession out of the blue by a distraught, angry or vindictive killer. Perry seldom relied on forensics. He counted on court-room confessions and he was inevitably rewarded. No mess. Danny wondered what it would be like with no mess. He wouldn't like it. No challenge. He loved his job.

"We wish," Lindsay said.

"He was a popular guy," said Danny.

"Not with everyone," said Lindsay.

4

Dr. Sid Hammerbeck pursed out his lower lip and looked over the top of his glasses at the corpse of Patricia Mycrant on the autopsy table. Mac stood at his side as the medical examiner probed with gloved hands and tools.

"Interesting," he said, pausing to bite his lower lip.

"What?" asked Mac.

"Eleven discernible wounds and some vaginal damage so extensive that I'm not sure yet how many cuts and tears there are. Your killer was very angry or very crazy or both. Blade of the knife is three inches. Fold up. Carry it in a pocket. It's sharp. Very sharp. As sharp as one of my scalpels. The owner of this knife has treated it lovingly."

Sid washed down the naked body with a stream of water from the hose next to the table.

There are generally three types of wounds caused by a knife: a beveled wound made by a blade entering the flesh at less than a right angle; a scrimmage wound caused by a twisting motion of the blade after it is in the flesh; and an oval-shaped wound made by a blade entering the flesh at a right angle. Patricia Mycrant's body bore all three types of wounds.

"What else can you tell me about the knife?" Mac asked.

"The blade nicked the pelvic bone three times," said Hammerbeck. "Punctured the spleen and liver. Impressions taken from the bones and organs should help identify the size and shape of the blade. I think I can give you enough to identify the specific knife from small indentations on the blade. Almost as good as a fingerprint."

"You've got something else," said Mac.

The ME looked down at the body and said, "Residue in the wounds, not much, but enough. I've bagged and sealed it for you. What it is I do not know."

Mac had already taken blood samples and the Starbucks cup to Jane Parsons in the DNA lab. The lab had been busy. It was always busy. The lab and the City of New York had resisted what so many other crime scene units across the country had done, sending their evidence to private labs. Time was a factor, but so was money.

Jane had promised to do the DNA testing as soon as possible and to run it through CODIS, the national DNA matching system, but first the DNA had to be extracted and analyzed. Television had created the illusion that testing could be done in a few hours or overnight. The truth was that even three days on a high-profile case was pushing the clock, depending on how many tests were scheduled and the availability of scientists. Mac also knew that it was possible, just possible and seldom done, to do a DNA test in as little as three or four hours. The use of a genetic analyzer had sped up the actual DNA test time.

But before the DNA is run through the analyzer, it has to be extracted by placing the evidence material in a vial and adding a chemical to separate the DNA from the surrounding material. Then the DNA is replicated so the scientist has more than one piece to test. The DNA is then placed into the genetic analyzer, which has ninety-six tiny wells into which scientists inject the DNA. The wells are in a rectangular block of plastic, twelve rows of eight wells. Positioned just above the wells is a row of needle-size capillaries. When the wells are filled, the scientist closes the machine and turns it on. The capillaries are then dipped into the first row of wells, where they draw up the DNA and send it into the machine. A laser light then picks out the different-size DNA particles as they pass by. The smaller pieces shoot by first, followed by the heavier, larger pieces. The result, an electropherogram, is recorded in a series of peaks, or alleles, which look like the readout on an electrocardiogram.

Jane had a lot of work to do before Mac could get any DNA results.

"Lunch in my office?" Jane had asked.

"If I can get away," he said.

"Can I lure you with pastrami on a kaiser with mustard and a pickle? On me?"

"Who could resist," he had said with a smile.

But now Mac watched Patricia Mycrant's blood wash away on the autopsy table in front of the medical examiner. Stubborn clots clung to the steel.

"Have you ever eaten Festivo Pollo Con Carne Dolce?" asked Sid.

Sid had been a successful chef for years after giving up his medical practice. No one, perhaps not even Dr. Sid Hammerbeck, knew why he had returned to medicine, why he had chosen to become a medical examiner.

"Can't say that I have," said Mac.

"I'll be happy to prepare it for you sometime," said Sid, carefully eyeing the pale corpse as he continued to wash it down.

"Thanks," said Mac.

"The trick is in the marinade," said Sid. "Marinate it too briefly and it fails to penetrate the flesh. Marinate too long and the spices overwhelm the texture of the bird."

"Fascinating," said Mac.

Sid reached down and moved Patricia Mycrant's left arm to expose the single wound in her armpit.

"This wound, almost surgically placed," he said, "dropped and nearly paralyzed her."

Mac looked at the medical examiner and said, "He knew what he was doing."

Sid nodded and continued hosing down the body.

"Ah, what have we here," he said, aiming the water at a clot along the left thigh.

Remnants of blood peeled away to reveal something deep red carved into the flesh.

"One more mystery," said Sid.

Mac leaned in closer.

"Or a clue," said Mac.

Cut into the dead woman's inner thigh was a distinct letter *D.*

In the small basement of the Wallen School, Bill Hexton sat in front of a black-and-white screen. Danny and Lindsay stood behind him.

Hexton looked less like a security guard than a student playing dress-up in tan slacks, a blue blazer and a loose-fitting blue and brown Wallen School tie.

"Been here long?" asked Danny.

"Not counting the six years I was a student at Wallen," Hexton said, "it's been three years. After I graduated, three years in the army, military police and then a little time in intelligence. Then right back here."

Hexton looked military. Super-close-cropped haircut, clean shaven, shoulders back.

Images drifted by on the screen, corridors, gymnasium, a dining hall.

"No bathrooms," said Hexton. "Privacy issues. No classrooms. Academic freedom issues. You can see the images roll from one camera to the next. We've got sixteen cameras. We can't afford to record all sixteen all the time so we roll from one to the other."

Both Lindsay and Danny knew the routine, but they listened patiently and watched the screen.

"There," said Hexton. "That's the corridor outside the chem lab just before nine this morning."

"Slow it down," said Danny, leaning in closer.

Hexton turned a knob on the console. Students, gray figures, moved in both directions down the hall. Some students started to enter the chemistry lab.

"Freeze that," said Danny.

Hexton pressed a button. The image stopped moving.

"Can you identify the students going into the room?"

"Sure. But we know who was in the class," said Hexton.

"Humor me," said Danny.

Hexton shrugged, pointed to the students about to enter the classroom and identified each of them.

"Okay," said Danny.

Hexton pressed a button and the image shifted to another corridor, another classroom, moving at normal speed.

"Can you jump forward, show the chem lab corridor and door when the class ended?" asked Danny.

"No problem," said Hexton. "Class would have ended at ten to ten, but Havel dismissed them halfway into the class."

"You know why?" asked Lindsay.

Hexton shook his head "no" as he watched images flash by, then slowed the tape down just before the white numbers at the top of the screen said nine-twenty.

The tape showed four students coming out of the lab. Then the image switched to the dining hall, where students were starting to trickle in.

"Find the next tape of the chem lab corridor," said Danny.

Hexton found it. The corridor was empty. The chem lab door was closed. Hexton found tapes of the corridor for the next half hour and then the image of Wayne O'Shea entering the lab.

"O'Shea says he fainted," said Lindsay.

"He could be lying," said Danny.

"Good actor? He knew the camera might be on him," said Lindsay. "I don't see any blood on him."

"I can't see O'Shea doing it," said Hexton.

"I knew a ninety-pound, eighty-two-year-old Baptist Sunday school teacher named Eloise Pringleman who'd never raised her voice to anyone," said Danny. "One morning a large, young deliveryman with a small shipment of fax machine paper for the church used the word 'fuck' as a recurring adjective. Eloise asked him to stop. He didn't. Eloise picked up a pair of very sharp scissors and created one of the bloodiest crime scenes I've ever seen. We'd like to take your tapes from this morning."

"I should check with the headmaster," said Hexton. "Student privacy issues."

"No one outside of our lab is going to see them. You gonna make us get a warrant?" asked Danny.

"Guess not," said Hexton. "I'll tell the headmaster. Anything else I can do?"

"Find the students who were in Havel's class this morning and bring them to the dining hall," said Danny. "One at a time. And I'd like the files on all of them, as well as on O'Shea."

"Lining up the students, no problem. Files? I'll need the headmaster's okay on that."

"Do what you can," said Danny.

"I'll take the tape," said Lindsay.

Hexton stretched and nodded.

"Where's the headmaster?" asked Danny.

"Damage control," said Hexton. "Students' parents. Alumni. Havel's widow. And reporters, not yet but soon. It's a mess."

"What can you tell us about Havel?"

"I had him for chemistry. Good teacher. Kept it interesting. Students liked him. He liked the students, seemed to be constantly amused by us. With some of the other teachers who were still around from when I was a student, it felt a little funny sort of being one of them, but Alvin made me feel comfortable, not just polite comfortable, but really comfortable from the first day. We had coffee, lunch once in a while. I'll miss him. Not just me. The teachers, staff, everyone liked him."

"Not everyone," said Danny.

In the student dining hall, Danny sat alone at a heavy wooden table, a Wallen School coffee cup in front of him, his tape recorder out, his open kit at his side. The lights were dim. The place reminded him of something out of Harry Potter.

The first student was sent in. Danny motioned for her to sit across from him. Danny wasn't comfortable. He had gone to a public school where there was a cafeteria, not a dining room, and the tables had been metal and benches had been bolted to the floor. At his school, the signs of teenage rage and rebellion had been evident in the obscenities scratched on benches and tabletops. There were no signs of even minor desecration in the Wallen School dining room.

"Annette Heights," Danny said, motioning to the chair across from him. "Mind if I tape our conversation?"

"No," she said.

Danny had turned on the machine the moment she entered the room.

"Good. Then talk to me."

The girl wore a green skirt and white blouse. Her face, round, younger looking than her fifteen years, was tinged with makeup. Her hair was wavy, black, long.

"And say what?" she asked, sitting down across from him. She didn't appear intimidated or nervous.

"Mr. Havel."

"I hear he's dead," she said calmly.

"You were in his AP chemistry class this morning."

"Yes."

"His body was found a few minutes after class let out," said Danny. "Hard to miss a murder taking place inside the classroom."

"Impossible," she said. "He was fine when the chime sounded and when I left the room. I was the first one out."

"Who was behind you?"

"I don't remember."

"Who else was in the class?"

She shrugged.

"Karen Reynolds the Goddess. James Tuvekian."

"The Goddess?"

"Have you met her?" asked the girl.

"Not yet."

"She holds the state record in the one hundred meter."

"Dash?"

"Water," she said. Annette did a mock swimming stroke and then settled back, arms folded.

"How was Mr. Havel?"

"Himself," she said. "No. Come to think of it, he wasn't. Or maybe that's just me exercising my imagination because he's dead."

"How was he?" asked Danny.

"How *wasn't* he," she said. "No bounce. He was a bouncer. Not today. And he let us out early."

"Why?"

"He didn't say."

Danny nodded.

"What did you think of Mr. Havel?"

"Alvin was much beloved," she said flatly, looking across the dining hall at the rain running down the windows.

"You didn't like him?"

She turned her eyes from the window and focused on Danny. "You're cute."

"Thank you," he said. "You didn't like Mr. Havel?"

"He was all right."

"Would you like to give me your hand?" he said with a smile.

She smiled back and held out one hand. He took it.

"Both of them," he said.

She held out her other hand. Danny removed a sheet of plastic from his kit and a spray can. He sprayed her palms and placed them on the plastic sheet. Then he took out his portable ALS and shield and examined her palms.

The process seemed to amuse her.

"See anything?" she asked.

"I'll let you know," he said.

"I want to know now," she demanded, no longer sounding amused.

"I guess I'm not so cute anymore," he said bagging the plastic sheet.

"None of this is legal," Annette said, folding

her arms. "I'm only fifteen. You didn't ask me if I wanted a lawyer."

"You aren't a suspect. You're a possible witness," said Danny. "Maybe next time we talk you'll want your parents or a lawyer."

"Now I'm a suspect?" she snapped, standing.

"A person of interest," he said.

"Do you know who my father is?" she asked.

"No," he said calmly. "Tell me."

"Robert Heights," she said.

"And . . . ?"

"You don't know who my father is?" she said, looking around the room for an unseen someone who could share with her this incredible moment in which she had encountered the one person in the civilized world who didn't know who Robert Heights was.

"Doesn't ring a bell," said Danny.

"This is unbelievable," she said. "My father is one of the ten greatest concert pianists who ever lived."

"That a fact?" said Danny.

"This is . . ."

"Want to tell me who killed Mr. Havel?"

"I don't know," she shouted.

"Have a nice day," said Danny. "Stay dry."

Annette Heights, cute and petite and used to getting what she wanted when she flashed her father's name, stalked out of the dining room.

Lindsay almost collided with her as she left.

"You didn't make a great impression on the little lady," she said, sitting across from Danny in the seat Annette had vacated.

"The Messer charm failed me," he said. "Girl's father is Robert Heights."

"Really?"

"Absolutely," said Danny. "I saw him in Carnegie Hall last year. I've got two of his CDs if you ever want to come by and listen. Schumann, Beethoven. As good as it gets."

"I'll borrow them," she said.

"They don't leave my apartment. Too precious," he said with a grin.

"The girl?"

"No blood on her hands," he said.

"But?"

"She's still a person of interest."

Stella scratched a bloody three-inch wound on her right ankle as she balanced her way toward the spot where Sheldon Hawkes had disappeared. She ignored the scratch, even though in some recess of her mind she knew she might have lost the ankle bracelet given to her by a friend, a friend she had thought might become more of a friend but hadn't. She had given him up. Maybe it was time to give up the bracelet too.

She was aware of Devlin moving past her.

She was aware of the pain in her ankle.

She was aware of the rain beating against her yellow disposable poncho with CSI FORENSIC LAB printed in black on the back.

A few yards from the spot where she had last seen Hawkes, Devlin's voice exploded, "Stop."

Stella stopped. She could hear fragments of plaster and wood tumbling into the hole she could now make out ahead of her.

"Careful," said Devlin, coming around the hole and touching her arm.

Below them was a pit about the size of a giant truck tire. The hole was dark.

"Hawkes," Stella called.

A light flashed on about ten feet down.

"Here," Hawkes said, his voice a damp echo.

"We'll get you out," said Devlin. "Hang in there."

Devlin had a large flashlight in his hand. He turned it on, knelt, and cast the beam downward. More of what had once been the floor of Doohan's slipped down into the hole.

Devlin's beam found Hawkes about a dozen feet below. The fireman cast the light along the inside of the hole and then back to Hawkes. Then he stood up and said softly to Stella, "He's in a basement. Sides of this thing are loose. Could implode if we touch them and—"

"Bury Hawkes," said Stella.

"It gets worse," he said. "There's a support beam

down there. You can take a look. It's on its side holding up a section of ceiling. It could go if we touch it."

By this time two more firemen had joined them at the hole.

"It'll be okay," said Devlin. "What do I call him?"

"Doctor Hawkes," said Stella.

"Doctor?"

"He's an MD," she said.

"Check," said Devlin, motioning the other two firemen back. He leaned over near the hole and said, "Doctor Hawkes, we'll rig something up. Don't try to climb up and don't touch that wooden beam to your left."

"Right," said Hawkes. "How long will this take?"

"Not sure," said Devlin. "We can't move too quickly. Anything we can do for you?

"Stop the rain," Hawkes said. "I'm up to my ankles in water and it's rising."

"How fast?" asked Devlin.

"Not sure. I'm not worried about myself."

"What do you mean?" Stella called.

"I'm not alone," yelled Hawkes. "There's a man trapped down here, with one of his legs pinned down by that beam."

"Alive?" asked Stella.

"Alive."

"Is he on his stomach or back?"

"His back."

"The water?" asked Stella.

"To his armpits," said Hawkes.

Something shifted in the debris. Across from Stella and Devlin a small avalanche of rubble rumbled down the hole. It drummed against the concrete basement floor.

"Hawkes, you all right?" Stella yelled.

"I am. He isn't."

"You have your kit?"

"I don't . . . yes. There it is."

Behind Stella, Devlin was giving orders to the other two firemen.

"Can he talk?" asked Stella.

Muffled sounds from below. A crack of thunder from the east.

The two firemen hurried away, moving toward their truck parked on Catherine.

"He can talk," said Hawkes.

Hawkes shined his flashlight on the face of the trapped man. He was white, probably in his late forties, lean, salt-and-pepper hair, military cut. He was wearing a leather jacket, now torn at the sleeve, and a drenched green turtleneck shirt.

"You all right?" Hawkes asked the man.

"Couldn't be better," said the man with a pained grin and a slight accent Hawkes couldn't quite place. "Legs pinned down, water rising, world about to come down on my head. Who could ask for more?"

"I'm a doctor," said Hawkes, gently touching the man's ribs and arms, and then his pinioned ankle. "Anything feel broken?"

"Ankle, maybe."

"You've got a few lacerations and bruises, nothing serious. Did you hit your head?"

"No, I always talk this way," the man said. "Name is Connor Custus. Easy to remember. Hard to forget."

He held out his right hand. Hawkes took it. The two end fingers were missing. Hawkes could feel the rough calluses on the man's palm.

"Scottish?" asked Hawkes.

"Australian," said Custus. "I guess I really know the meaning of being down under now."

"We'll get out. FDNY is working on it." Hawkes reached for his kit and opened it.

"How's a doctor happen to be at the scene of an explosion?"

"Crime Scene Investigation," said Hawkes, carefully touching the man's trapped right ankle, which was almost covered by water.

Custus winced and bit his lower lip.

Hawkes tried the other ankle. No reaction.

"Right one broken?" asked Custus.

"Yes," said Hawkes.

"Can you set it?"

"I'd rather get you out of here first."

"The precarious state of this dungeon might

make timely escape unlikely," said Custus. "Edmond Dantès had more to work with than we have and he had the use of both legs and no rising water."

"Are you in pain?" asked Hawkes.

"On a scale of one to ten? I'll give it a seven, but I've been close to nine in my day. You have something that will take the edge off in your box of tricks there?"

"Yes."

"Then by all means administer to a body and soul in distress."

Hawkes pulled a plastic bottle of Vicodin out of the kit. Being able to carry prescription painkillers in case of a situation like this one was one of the advantages of being both a physician and a CSI.

Hawkes could hear the rain rush through cracks and fissures above him, threatening the fragile, sagging ceiling.

"You were in the bar?" asked Hawkes.

"I was," said Custus, downing the pill Hawkes handed him. "Driven in by the rain for a morning wake-up beer and winding up in a hole as ominous as any of Dante's pits. Poetically and metaphorically that would make you my Beatrice."

"Do you remember what happened?" asked Hawkes, shining the beam of the flashlight into Custus's eyes. The pupils constricted normally.

Hawkes perched the flashlight on a flat rusted

square of iron next to the injured man. Its light was crime-scene bright. The waterproof flashlight had a battery life of one hundred hours. Luckily, Hawkes had put in new batteries two days ago.

"It's an odd story and I'm given to making my stories lengthy," said Custus as Hawkes opened the man's shirt to examine him for other bruises or trauma.

"Not too lengthy, I hope," said Hawkes.

"Ah yes, the tide is rising," said Custus with a grin, "and we await the shadow of an albatross.

"I was sitting at the bar, talking to a man I had just met when—"

The ceiling shifted. The beam moved a fraction, pinning Custus even more tightly. He let out a pained groan.

"Hawkes?" Stella called from above.

"We're here," said Hawkes.

Custus's chest was a map of scars, most of them old, pink, hardened.

"Football, Australian rules," Custus explained. "Rough and tumble. Lots of biting, scratching and the rare but distinctive spitting. Fun for one and all."

Custus was grinning. Hawkes didn't grin back. Custus's scars were not the result of football injuries. He'd seen these kinds of scars before.

And then Hawkes saw it. Under folds of his clinging wet shirt and a smudge of oily filth, he saw it.

"You were sitting at the bar talking to a man you had just met," prompted Hawkes.

"Right, well—"

"Who shot you?"

"Shot me?" asked Custus.

"You've been shot," said Hawkes. "Don't you feel it?"

"Not really. A little stiffness there, but nothing like the heroic agony of my broken ankle. How bad is it?"

"I don't know," said Hawkes. "We'll get you out of here to a hospital."

"It doesn't have to hurt to kill you," said Custus.

"No, it doesn't," Hawkes said, leaning over with his flashlight to examine the wound, out of which, Hawkes could now see, blood pumped steadily.

5

THE BODY OF JAMES FELDT was discovered by a woman named Annabeth Edwards. "Discovered" might suggest that she had either stumbled upon or been searching for the body. In actuality, she couldn't miss it as she made her way through the nooks and crannies of Strutts, McClean & Berg. The door to one of the offices was open, wide open and waiting for her to push it. She did. The room was painted red with blood and the body that lay sprawled next to the desk had its pants pulled down to reveal a horror of mutilation.

To her credit, Annabeth did not drop her bag, which contained a lemon poppy muffin and a coffee sweetened with cream and three packets of Equal. Annabeth didn't recognize the man with granny glasses dangling from one ear. She'd only been at her job for two weeks. She was here on this shit of a day to make an impression, to impress any partner who might happen in, deciding that there was something in the office worth the risk of being swept away by the deluge outside.

She stood in the doorway, hands at her side, knowing enough not to go in or touch anything. It wasn't necessary to see if the man might still be alive. He obviously was not.

It struck her that whoever had done this might still be here. She stood silently, listening. Just the rain pounding against the blood-streaked window over the head of the dead man.

"This is what I get for being a loyal employee," she said aloud, moving back into the reception area, placing her bag on a desk and reaching for a phone.

Then, and only then, did she remember the man in the downstairs lobby who, head down, had walked out as she had come in. Their eyes had met. He had nodded. So had she.

Annabeth took out her cell phone and made the call. The woman at 911 took it, forwarded it. A pair of uniforms who were on their fourteenth hour on the job threw away their cups of coffee and drove the six blocks to the scene of the crime.

The report of the killing reached the computer screen at CSI headquarters about an hour after Annabeth Edwards had called it in.

"Look at this," Mac said.

Flack looked over his shoulder at the screen.

"'Genital mutilation,'" Flack read.

"Like Patricia Mycrant," said Mac.

"A stretch. Someone murders a woman on a rooftop on Eighty-second and then runs to an office building in midtown to carve up a guy in an office?"

"I've got a feeling," said Mac, sitting back.

"Me too. I've got a feeling we're on our way to look at a dead man."

James Tuvekian, whose father was a neurosurgeon, was tall and almost anorexically thin. He sat in the dining hall of the Wallen School, wearing khakis and a tan-and-yellow striped button-down polo shirt and a smile. Not a smirk, not a smile of amusement, but the smile of someone who had learned to wear a mask.

"What did you see, James?" Danny asked.

James pursed his lips and shrugged. "You mean in Mr. Havel's classroom?"

"No, at the movies last night," said Danny.

"Not funny," said James.

"Not funny," Danny agreed.

"What did I see? Nothing. Mr. Havel was behind the table setting something up on the microscope. We filed out. End of episode."

"Someone killed him."

"I heard. He let us out early."

"Why?"

"Who knows? Maybe he wanted to play with himself. Karen Reynolds is in that class. He had a thing for her. Don't think he did anything about it, but he looked and panted."

"What about you?"

"You mean Karen?" James said. "I look. Who doesn't?"

"Red pencils," said Danny, placing the red pencils on the wooden table.

"I see," said James.

"Who uses them?"

"Mr. Havel. Anyone who wanted them, or the markers, or the highlighters, could take them."

"Ever arm wrestle?" asked Danny.

"What for?"

"Fun." Danny grinned and put his arm on the table.

"You are one strange cop. No, thanks."

"You work out?"

"No."

"Okay. Give me your hands."

Danny checked his palms. When he was finished, James rose from his seat.

"We'll talk again," Danny said.

"I'm looking forward to it."

"Send Karen in when you leave," said Danny. "And don't talk to her."

"I don't talk to her. She doesn't talk to me. That way our love will always be a mystery."

"'Bells Are Ringing,'" said Danny.

"You like show tunes?" said the boy.

"My musical taste is eclectic," said Danny.

"Anything else?" asked James.

"We've got trouble right here in River City."

"Yeah," said the boy. "Remember the Maine, Plymouth Rock and The Golden Rule."

Danny adjusted his glasses and nodded as the boy left the dining hall.

As he waited for the next student, he wondered how Hawkes was doing. Stella had called and briefed him on the situation, had said the fire department had assured her they would get him out. Danny thought she had sounded less than completely confident. He'd told her to call him if she needed anything, wished he could do more.

Moments later Karen Reynolds came in and sat down without being asked.

Danny had expected a petite blond high school bombshell, like Shirley Moretti from when he was in high school. Karen Reynolds was blond, but not like Shirley Moretti. Her hair, cut short, was, like Karen Reynolds, fresh. She was lean and solid and tall, with long legs, and wore no makeup. There was an aura of health and wholesomeness about her. Karen Reynolds belonged in California on the beach or in Montana climbing a mountain.

"You swim?" Danny asked as she sat, back straight, showing blue eyes and perfect white teeth.

"Yes," she said.

"Records?" he said.

"A few. You swim?"

"Didn't have a pool at my school. I swam in the river."

"The river? The Hudson?"

"I kept my mouth closed," he said.

She smiled.

"What did you see in Mr. Havel's class before he dismissed you?"

"Nothing unusual."

"You liked Mr. Havel?"

"Yes," she said.

"And he liked you."

It was a statement, not a question. She said nothing.

"You were the last one out?"

"Yes. I think so."

"No one was left in the classroom besides Mr. Havel."

"No one," she said.

"I'm curious. What does your father do?"

"My father is dead," she said.

"I'm sorry."

"It's all right. He died when I was seven. He was a diamond dealer, very heavily insured. My mother took over the business."

"Mr. Havel ever make any moves on you?"

"No," she said. "He looked. That's all. I liked him. He was a great teacher."

"You have a boyfriend?"

"You asking for a date?"

She was smiling, maybe trying to make Danny a little uncomfortable.

"I'll wait a few years," he said. "You have a boyfriend?"

"Terry Rucker. A senior. Terry is not the jealous type and he did not come to school today. He's stuck in Ithaca. Rain. Basketball game last night."

Danny nodded.

"I'd like to call my mother before I say anything else."

"You're eighteen. We don't need your mother's permission to talk to you."

"You didn't tell me I could leave any time I wish unless you're arresting me."

"Why should we arrest you?" asked Danny. "You kill Mr. Havel?"

"No."

The answer was forceful. Danny was starting to think she was taller than he was.

"We can hold you on suspicion of withholding information," he said.

"There is no such charge."

"You planning on becoming a lawyer?"

"Yes," she said.

Danny was certain now. The girl was taller than he was.

He examined her palms, which she allowed him to do without protest. "You can leave," he said when he was done.

"No," she said. "I want to cooperate. So if you have more questions . . ."

"No, you can leave."

She stood. So did Danny. He didn't normally stand when women came or went, but there was something about her that made him sure that she expected the gesture. She took a dozen steps toward the dining hall door, then stopped and turned around.

"Everybody liked Mr. Havel," she said.

"Not everybody," Danny said.

Lindsay had laid a white cloth on the floor of the room in the CSI lab. On the table in front of her was a large, dead pig. Next to the dead pig were two hollow-cast, human-shaped heads lined on the inside with blood packs. One of the heads was vertical, head up. The other was horizontal, on its side.

Lindsay wore a white lab coat and goggles and her hair was covered in a plastic surgery-room cover.

She was ready. Different-size sharpened red pencils were lined up on the lab table. Lindsay picked up one of the thicker pencils in her gloved hand and plunged it into the neck of the pig. There was no blood. The blood had been drained from the pig the previous day. She left the pencil in the pig's neck and consulted the crime scene photographs of Alvin Havel and her own notes on the depth of his neck wound.

She shook her head, pulled the pencil from the pig, selected another pencil and plunged that one in, harder than the first time. Again she consulted the photos and her notes. Closer. Very close, but not quite right. She repeated the process once more, plunging the pencil in even harder. This time it was almost perfect. She removed the pencil and inserted a needlepoint gauge in the wound.

When she looked at the reading, she chewed on her lower lip and made a notation. Whoever had stabbed Alvin Havel had been strong, very strong.

The pig was on a stainless steel wheeled cart. Lindsay opened the door, wheeled the cart out of the room and turned it over to lab tech Chad Willingham, who was waiting eagerly outside the door for news.

Lindsay showed him her notes.

She started back into the room to assault the blood-packed heads on the table.

"Can I . . . ?" Chad asked.

"Sure," said Lindsay.

There was about to be a lot of blood in the room, and someone would have to clean it up. That someone would be Chad. He at least deserved to be in on the fun part.

Sid Hammerbeck was looking down at the body of Alvin Havel. The pencils embedded in the chemistry teacher's eye and neck were still there. Sid removed the pencils carefully, noting the depth of each wound. The only question was which of the wounds had killed the teacher and when.

Sid gently probed the eye wound. The wound was remarkably clean, a straight puncture. The victim had not squirmed or fought back. This was not a wild, frantic stab to the eye. The man was already dead when someone had plunged the pencil into his eye.

Sid consulted his notes and called Mac on his cell phone.

The line was busy.

"They think the ceiling's going to come down," Stella said into the cell phone.

She was sitting in the compact crime scene vehicle she and Hawkes had taken to the site of Doohan's Bar. The drumming of the rain on the roof made it difficult to hear. She clicked up the volume on her phone.

"When?" asked Mac. He was currently on the

elevator going up to the law offices of Strutts, McClean & Berg in the Stanwick Oil Building.

"They don't know. An hour, maybe," she said.

"What are they doing now?" Mac asked as the elevator stopped and he stepped out on the nineteenth floor.

"Running a hose into the basement to try to pump out some of the water."

Stella looked out the window at the group of firemen gathered around the sink hole. A hose from their truck ran across the debris and into the pit.

"You've got a gunshot victim at the scene?"

"It gets better," she said. "Victim's ankle is pinned under a heavy beam. Water's slowly rising in the pit and I get the feeling from Hawkes that the victim may not make it another forty-five minutes."

A policeman, raincoat open, stood in front of the outer door. Mac nodded at him and moved past.

"Anything you can do to help Hawkes?"

"No," Stella said. "It's up to the firemen. They're pumping water out of the hole."

"Is Hawkes in any danger?"

"These guys seem pretty confident they'll get him out with time to spare," she said. "I trust them."

"Keep me posted," said Mac.

He hung up. So did Stella. She had dead men to examine.

• • •

The reception area of the law offices was empty. Down a hall to the left Mac could see a second police officer, a heavyset veteran Mac recognized.

"Weaver," said Mac.

"Detective Taylor," Weaver replied.

"What do we have?" asked Mac.

"Dead man in there," Weaver said, nodding at an office to his left. Then, looking to his right, he said, "Woman who found the body is in an office over there. Dead man's James Feldt, accountant. Live woman is Annabeth Edwards."

Mac nodded, put on his gloves and entered the office where James Feldt's body awaited him.

Weaver didn't follow. There was nothing in there he wanted to see again. In his seventeen years on the streets, Weaver had seen bad, really bad. The scene in Feldt's office was definitely on his top five list.

Mac scanned the room, put down his kit, took out his camera and began to take photos. The first one he took was of the area on the floor in front of him where he would have to walk. There was blood. Lots of blood. Mac moved in. More footprints. Weaver's bootmarks were clear. They went up to the body where Weaver must have confirmed what he'd known the second he entered the room, that James Feldt was dead. There were other prints, about a size nine. Mac leaned over to take close-ups of them.

When he finished photographing the room and the body, Mac put the camera away and looked down at the dead man. Like the woman on the roof, Patricia Mycrant, Feldt had been mutilated, his genitals cut off after his pants were pulled down.

Mac checked under the man's right arm, then his left. He found the wound under the left arm almost exactly where Patricia Mycrant had been stabbed.

Mac took the dead man's temperature and then rolled him slightly on his side to check for lividity. The man had been dead for at least two hours.

Kneeling, cotton swab in hand, Mac carefully rubbed blood away from the inside of the dead man's thigh. He found what he was looking for in almost the exact spot it had been on Patricia Mycrant. The only difference was that the letter carved in the corpse was an *A* instead of a *D*.

"Now what?" asked Connor Custus, looking up in the direction of the bustle of firemen.

The water level had risen about half an inch more and creaking sounds came from the darkness.

Hawkes had slowed the blood flow from the bullet wound in Custus's side with gauze pads. Now he was examining Custus's hands and body.

"It's my leg that's broken," Custus said. "And

my abdomen that's been shot. While the rest of me may not be prime, it is still, I believe, functioning at par."

Hawkes took an aerosol can from his kit and sprayed both of Custus's palms and the webbing between his thumbs and forefingers. Then he examined both hands under his portable ALS.

"Ah, I just figured out what you're looking for," said Custus

Hawkes didn't respond.

Custus pulled his hand away and let it fall into the water. He did the same with his other hand.

"Ironic," said Custus. "This cursed rain may be the death of me, but if it isn't, it will wipe away a few of my many sins."

"Gunshot residue doesn't come off that easily," said Hawkes. "And you don't have to have fired the weapon to have molecular traces of metal. You just have to have handled it."

"I know," said Custus. "And should we survive I'll explain to all as I explain to you. I fired at a range in Erie, Pennsylvania, yesterday. It's my wont as I travel to stop from time to time to retain my skills."

"And you need these skills . . ." Hawkes began.

"I'm a freelance bill collector," Custus said. "I specialize in face-to-face discussions with those in debt for large sums. From time to time one of the delinquents is unreasonable. I've never had to shoot anyone, for which I thank Saints Peter and Paul and my own professional persuasive powers."

"If there's a pattern on the gun handle, and there usually is," said Hawkes, "traces of it can show up on the hand."

"Then it would be essential to have the weapon, would it not?" asked Custus.

A tumble of plaster joined the rain and a black tube snaked down the the wall of the sinkhole.

"You see it?" Devlin called from above.

"Yes," called Hawkes. "I've got it."

"Put it in the water," called Devlin, "and find something to keep it down."

"Right," called Hawkes.

"Do not pull on the hose," warned Devlin. "Just guide it and tell me when it's under the water level."

Hawkes did as instructed. "Got it," he shouted.

"We're going to pump slowly," said Devlin. "We don't want to set off vibrations. You understand?"

"I understand," said Hawkes.

He found a jutting twist of metal coils embedded in a concrete block. The hose fit between the metal coils. Hawkes managed to bend one of the coils so that the hose stayed in place, its head in the water.

"The scars on your body," Hawkes said to Custus.

"And on my arms and one right here on my neck," said Custus. His eyes were closed against the pain in his legs.

"They're not from Australian football games."

"No, they are not."

"Mind if I ask where they're from?"

"Yes," said Custus. "I don't want to be rude, but I do mind. Now, if you can do without me for a few minutes, I've got a thing I can do to ease the pain. Learned it in China. My ankle is numb, my body cold, my brow feverish and that mysterious bullet hole in my side is beginning to throb."

"China?"

"Lovely place to visit but I wouldn't recommend eating the cats and dogs. Too sinewy."

"You changed the subject," said Hawkes.

"I thought I did it rather skillfully," Custus said with a sigh. "All right. The scars. I don't like to talk about them. War wounds."

"Which war?"

"I'll keep that one to myself," Custus said with a smile.

"Burns," said Hawkes. "From explosions. Different explosions. The scars are from different times. Traces of the explosive material can be found in those scars, and judging from the color and healing rate, there were at least three different explosive materials."

"I've never had good luck," said Custus. "No, take that back. I'm still alive. I'd call that good luck, wouldn't you? I think I'll do my meditation thing now."

He was shutting down, or pretending to shut down.

"Is Detective Bonasera up there?" Hawkes yelled.

"I'll get her," called Devlin.

"I need to send something up to her."

"I don't think we should—" Devlin began.

"It's light, a digital photo clip. A string will be good enough."

Hawkes wiped the rain from his eyes. His legs were beginning to feel numb.

"Hawkes?" Stella called.

"I'm sending you pictures. Get them back to the lab and find someone who can check out the scars on the body of the man down here. His name is Connor Custus."

"You got it," Stella said.

Something moved behind him. Hawkes turned and saw Custus fling something into the darkness. Whatever it was made a splash and was gone.

"Dr. Hawkes," Custus said. "You are disturbing my meditation."

Custus was turned slightly and painfully on his side. Hawkes could see the blood-soaked gauze just above the water level. Hawkes reached into his kit and came up with a small black plastic object about the size of a hand-held flashlight. He flicked it on and placed it against Custus's stomach.

"I swear to you I am not pregnant."

Hawkes didn't answer. He pinpointed the metal

detector and slowly ran it across Custus's stomach and side. It let out a beep. Hawkes kept moving it around, getting more beeps till the beeping was almost furious. A flick and the metal detector went quiet.

"I think the bullet may be in or near your gall bladder or liver."

"But I shall survive?" he asked.

"If the bullet doesn't move. So far the flow of blood doesn't indicate a sudden rupture."

"But it could happen," said Custus.

"Yes."

"And you're considering going in there and getting the bullet out of my side."

"Yes," said Hawkes. "It can't stay where it is."

"You've removed bullets from organs in the past?"

"Yes," said Hawkes.

"Many?"

"Many."

What he didn't tell the pale Custus was that almost all the people from whose bodies he had retrieved bullets had been dead.

The last of the four students who had been in Alvin Havel's class that morning was Cynthia Parrish.

She walked across the floor of the dining hall, her shoes clacking in time to the beating of the rain on the windows. Danny had set the scene so that each student would have to take a long walk to the table. You could learn a lot by the way someone walked. This girl walked with bouncing confidence.

Cynthia Parrish was red haired, freckle faced and cute. Her teeth were white and her grin was simply perfect. She wore no makeup. Her navy blue skirt ended below her knees and her Wallen white sweatshirt was a size too large. She had pushed the sleeves up past her elbows.

Danny knew that Cynthia Parrish, a sophomore, was taking senior level and college credit courses and was easily the smartest student in the school. The file in front of him made that clear.

She sat with hands folded on her lap, waiting.

"Can I look at your hands?" he asked.

"You mean 'May I look at your hands,' right? I don't doubt that you have the ability to look at my hands."

"May I look at your hands?" Danny asked.

"Sure," she said, holding out her palms. "You'll find traces of chemicals, the same chemicals you'll find on the hands of the other students in Mr. Havel's class."

Danny examined her hands, took a scraping of residue from her palms and deposited it in a clear plastic bag.

"Any idea who killed Mr. Havel?" he asked.

"Sure," she said. "But I don't think I'll share it. I'm probably wrong and you asked if I had 'any idea.' 'Any idea' can get someone in trouble."

"You liked Mr. Havel?"

"Everyone liked Mr. Havel," she said. "He worked at being liked. He could have run for Congress and gotten the teen vote if teens could vote."

"But not your vote," Danny said, meeting the girl's eyes.

"Not my vote," she agreed, making a popping sound with her lips.

"Why's that?"

"You want me to speak ill of the dead."

"Just the truth will be fine."

"He made me uncomfortable. Like he was one of those pod people in *Invasion of the Body Snatchers*. You know, big smile and a kind word, but something was missing or lurking."

"Lurking?"

"I have a vivid imagination," she said with a shrug.

"Who was the last person to leave Mr. Havel's class?" asked Danny.

"Me," she said. "But anyone could have turned around and gone back. Want a suggestion?"

"Go ahead," Danny said.

"Check the clothes of everyone in that class for blood," she said.

"You too?"

"Why not?"

"Thanks for the suggestion."

"You're already doing that, aren't you, checking for blood I mean?"

He reached down into his kit on the floor and came up with a flashlight with a blue light. It was dark in the cafeteria, dark enough for the light to work. He turned it on and aimed it at her. Nothing.

"You change your clothes today?"

"No," she said.

"I can ask the other students," said Danny.

"You think they'd remember what I was wearing this morning? You've got the wrong girl."

"Okay, what about the others. Did they change clothes?"

"Don't remember," she said. "I think they're wearing the same things they had on in class, but then again, I haven't really been looking."

"You don't like them, do you? You're the smart kid. The others say things—"

"Detective," she said with a smile. "You've got the wrong school. This isn't inner city anti-nerd. I'm fine with the other kids, have lots of friends. My boyfriend is on the track team and I'm on the cross-country. Our school won the history, math and literature New York private school competition. I was captain, the youngest ever. Every one of the students were behind us. Strange as it may seem to you, I'm a popular girl."

"Every one of the students *was* behind us," said Danny, adjusting his glasses. "Every one is singular."

Cynthia Parrish smiled.

"Mr. Havel's dead," said Danny.

Cynthia Parrish's smile faded. "I know."

"What do you know?"

"He had trouble remembering his table of elements," she said. "He's been distracted for a while."

"How long?"

"A few months," she said.

"You know why?"

"No," she said. "But something changed. Something happened. He had trouble keeping his mind on the class. Seven times he asked me to take over the class. That was fine with me and the other students. He tried to make it look as if he wanted to give me the chance to teach. But that wasn't it. He just wasn't up to doing it."

"You want to be a teacher?" Danny asked.

"Not anymore," she said.

6

DJ RIGGS STOOD UNDERNEATH the doorway overhang of Rhythm & Soul Music on 125th in Harlem. The streets were clear, except for the few fools trying to make a dash for who-the-hell-knew-where, most of them eventually being pelted to the nearest doorway by the rain.

DJ smiled. The rain from hell was a gift. They would expect him to make a dash for the subway station. DJ was too smart for that.

DJ was twenty-seven, a two-time loser, last time for dealing. Two undercovers had broken into his crib less than fifteen minutes ago. DJ had made it out the window and down to the street and looked back knowing that a third and final stretch upstate was only a hundred yards behind. The undercovers might have been faster than he was and in better shape, but DJ was highly motivated.

He ran until the rain and his failing breath told him running was no longer an option. Rhythm & Soul had been there, not yet opened. Might not even be open later on a day like this.

DJ didn't pray for the rain to continue. If there was a God out there, DJ was definitely not on his good side. He wasn't bad enough for help from the devil either, at least he didn't think so. Ride out the rain. Stay off the street, out of sight. They would give up.

DJ heard a cry and wasn't sure what it was at first. Then he connected the cry with what he saw shuffling along the curb. A toddler, dark skinned, in diapers, crying, arms stretching out for someone who wasn't there. DJ couldn't tell if it was a boy or a girl.

He looked around, didn't see anyone. Where had this kid come from? Must have wandered off from his mother in the chaos of rain. The toddler was now about twenty feet in front of him.

Someone would come, DJ was sure. The kid was just getting wet, he wasn't hurt or anything. It was DJ who could be hurt if he tried to help. What good would he do? What could he do without getting caught?

Just wait. The baby toddled along. Then the horror hit DJ. He realized that the toddler had stepped off the curb and been knocked down by the rushing water in the gutter. The child was now being dragged along by the current toward an open drain whose mouth was definitely wide enough to welcome the child.

It was DJ's turn to cry out. He didn't even think, just ran from the doorway, watching the baby inch toward the drain, toward the sewer, toward the rats, the filth, no-doubt-about-it death.

DJ ran, almost crying, until he reached the child, right in front of the open gushing drain. He held tight to the baby's arms in spite of his slipping grip. He pulled the baby to him onto the sidewalk, felt its heart beating against his chest. When he opened his eyes he could see the two undercover cops splashing their way toward him in the middle of the street.

Leonard Giles, head of the tech lab, drove his wheelchair to the computer and keyed up the photographs Hawkes had taken of Custus. He had already run tests on the bits of wood and remnants of metal and plastic Stella had sent him.

"I think it was a bomb," Stella had said when she called. "More than one bomb."

"Someone wanted to blow up a bar?" Giles said.

"Looks that way," Stella said.

"Al Qaeda gone mad? Seeking unlikely targets to terrorize the nation?"

It wasn't funny and Stella didn't laugh. After a

long silence Stella said, "Hawkes may be trapped in a sinkhole with the bomber."

"I'll take care of it," Giles had said soberly.

Now he sat in front of the large computer screen. He typed in instructions and a geometric form appeared, a circle of Os and Cs with six H3Cs around them.

TATP, triacetone triperoxide, the explosive used in the London subway bombings, found in the shoe of Richard Reid, favored by Hamas, was highly unstable. The bomb maker, Giles knew, was almost as likely to blow himself up making it as he was to finish and deliver it. At least two bomb makers in Ireland had been victims of their own TATP bombs and more than forty bomb makers in Gaza and the West Bank had lost their lives to the unstable explosive.

TATP can be made of common household items such as drain cleaner, hydrogen peroxide and acetone.

Giles downloaded and saved the information, then inserted a CD. The information on the CD had been sent as an attachment from London and had been received less than half an hour ago. On the screen appeared a photograph of a man, his shirt off, his hair tousled, his left eye blackened. His chest was a jungle of hair parted by rivulets of scars, some white, some red, some ridged. The man's left hand was missing. Under the photograph of the man was information on the kind of explosive that had caused the scars. Next to the screen showing the CD were photographs Hawkes had taken of Custus. On the screen, the bare-chested Custus now appeared next to the redheaded man with one arm.

Giles moved slowly through the photographs on the CD that had been sent from London. He had no trouble finding a match for the scars, actually several matches. Giles concluded that the man in the pit with Hawkes was a survivor of at least four different kinds of bomb, including nitroglycerin and TATP.

"Definitely," Lindsay said.

She and Danny were standing in the laboratory with the blood-soaked heads Lindsay had been testing. One head was currently in almost the same position in which they had found Alvin Havel.

Lindsay, dissatisfied with commercial artificial blood, had developed her own formula that she constantly changed as she searched for the perfect texture and color.

Danny examined the blood splatters, looked at the crime scene photographs she had handed him and said, "Right."

"Blow to the neck came when he was standing, head up," she said. "Blow to the eye came when his head was on the desk."

"When he was dead," said Danny.

"Dead at least ten minutes. Sid agrees. No blood splatter from the eye wound. He was already dead."

"And your explanation?"

"One of those kids killed Havel, then waited around before stabbing him in the eye and leaving."

"Why?" he asked.

"We've got one really angry kid here."

"Not necessarily," said Danny.

Lindsay looked at him and waited. He took his mini–tape recorder out of his pocket.

"Wayne O'Shea, the kids call him Brody," said Danny.

"He's the one who found the body."

Danny clicked on the recorder. It whirred to the number Danny had remembered, stopped and began.

Danny: And no one was in the room or
        outside it when you went in?

O'Shea: No one.

Danny: What did you—?

O'Shea: I saw Alvin. I saw . . . I'll never
        forget what I saw.

Danny: And you were in your classroom the
        entire period?

O'Shea: Yes. I went in to ask Alvin about
        lunch and we'd heard this noise through
        the wall. So . . .

Danny: Do you know if he was having any
    trouble with any of the students or other
    teachers or parents?

O'Shea: Everyone liked Alvin. He was
    smart, a good teacher, maybe a great
    teacher. He won the Wallen Award, the
    Dorwenski Award, the Student Favorite
    Award, all the awards. The students
    admired him.

Danny: And you?

O'Shea: He was my best friend here. I'll miss
    him. I'll be haunted by what someone
    did to him.

Danny: What was the last time you saw him
    before you found him dead?

O'Shea: He was coming out of the closet.

Danny: He was gay?

O'Shea: No, a real closet, at the back of his
    laboratory behind the white board. The
    board slides. He used it as his storeroom.

Danny pushed a button. The tape recorder
stopped.

"You looked in the closet," Lindsay said.

"I looked in the closet."

Danny was smiling.

"Okay," Lindsay said. "What did you find?"

"Traces of blood."

• • •

The limping man stood outside the door and listened to the pacing footsteps and the occasional grumbled words inside the apartment. The hallway was dark and smelled of urine and rotting food.

He had entered the building through the lobby door, though it wasn't much of a lobby and it wasn't much of a door. He had stood outside, hooded against the rain, and looked up at the words HECHT ARMS cut into the gray stone over the door.

There were signs that someone at some time had dutifully replaced the broken lock on the lobby door. The wooden doorjamb was cracked, the broken lock loose in a door that just didn't give a damn any longer.

The lobby was just big enough to stand in and look at the eighteen mailboxes, some of which stood open, some of which were protected by small flimsy padlocks.

Some of the mailboxes bore names printed in black magic marker. Some had names scratched directly into the thin metal. Some bore no name at all.

He didn't need to find a name. He already knew the right apartment. He had been here before, once before. This visit would be very different.

There was an inner lobby door. No lock. He went in and walked down the first-floor hallway, weaving past a pile of newspapers in front of one door, a tricycle with a bent front wheel in front of another. Voices, vague, crying, someone shouting in anger, television sets droning relentlessly on, laughing, applauding.

The limping man paused in front of the door at the dark end of the hallway. He knocked. No answer, though he could hear muttering, pacing beyond the door. He knocked again, louder, much louder. The muttering stopped. The pacing stopped.

"Who is it? What the fuck do you want?" said a voice.

"Adam."

Silence beyond the door.

Then it opened a few inches.

"Adam?"

Timothy Byrold opened the door wider and looked at his visitor. Timothy, shirtless in a baggy pair of dirty white painter's overalls, needed a shave and a strong comb. He was big, taller than the limping man by three inches, heavier by twenty-five pounds. Timothy seemed to sense the man's disapproval and ran a hand through his thick hair. It did nothing except make the dirty hair stand up. He looked like a clown about to put on his makeup. The image did not strike the limping man as funny.

"What are you doing here?" asked Timothy.

"Can I come in?"

"It's not fit out there for man nor beast," said Timothy, stepping back.

The limping man stepped in and shut the door behind him.

The studio apartment looked very much as it had the other time he had been here, cot in a corner with the sheet untucked, a single sweat-stained pillow, a rough khaki blanket in a tangle, a sagging sofa that had once been orange but was now a sooty burnt bark color, a small wooden table with two chairs, a battered chest of drawers with a small color television on top of it. A refrigerator sat near the only window.

On the table was a bowl. In the bowl was a mound of what looked like soggy Cheerios. The cereal was being probed by a single, large black fly.

The room was as repulsive as the man.

"It's raining like shit out there," Timothy said. "Like shit. I'm stuck in here, in here. And the TV's broken. It's like being in a cell. You know what I mean?"

"Yes."

"I'm used to wandering, finding things, meeting people," said Timothy, rubbing his face.

"I know."

"Hell of a time for a visit," said Timothy. "Hell of a time."

Timothy picked up three magazines from the sofa and dropped them on the floor in a corner to give his guest a place to sit. Then he turned and tried to smile.

"I've got a couple of Cokes."

"No, thanks."

"So, have a seat."

"No, thanks."

"Then what, what?"

"You ever make a promise?"

"A promise. Yeah, sure. I must have. Everybody makes promises," said Timothy, noticing, sensing that something was odd about his visitor.

"Did you keep your promises?"

"Some, I guess. Don't remember."

Timothy sat on the sofa and looked up. Then he saw what was wrong. His visitor was wearing white, skin-tight gloves.

"I made a promise," the limping man said.

"Interesting," said Timothy. "Sure you don't want a Coke? Sure you don't want to start making sense or get the hell out of here?"

"Remember, I know what you are."

"And I know what you are," said Timothy. "So what? That's what you came to talk about? You need a shoulder to cry on? We've got a place for that, remember? Once a week, remember?"

"I remember."

The limping man moved toward the sofa. Timothy rose. He didn't like the blank look on his visitor's face.

"Get the hell out," Timothy said. "Or say something interesting that makes sense."

He took another step forward. Timothy stood, legs apart, hands ready. He was no stranger to violence. There were times when he welcomed it. He expected no problem in throwing out this intruder. He reached for the limping man's poncho.

The limping man ducked and in a crouch came up with a knife in his right hand. He stepped forward, flowing into the move and plunged the blade under Timothy's armpit, burying it to the hilt.

Timothy grunted, not sure of what had happened, thinking he had been punched, losing his breath. He reached for the limping man's hair, but the man knocked his hand away with an elbow and delivered a short, sudden chop to Timothy's neck.

Timothy went down with a moan, reaching out for something to grab, to hold him up. The pain under his arm had spread to his chest. He was sitting now, puzzled, dazed. He looked up at his visitor who kicked him in the chest. Timothy went to the floor on his back, panting, trying to catch his breath.

"You . . . you're . . . my only friend," Timothy whispered.

"Not anymore. Not ever."

Timothy felt the straps of his overalls being pulled down. Then he felt the overalls being pulled off.

"What?" he managed. "Why?"

"You know."

When the next wave of pain came, Timothy wanted to scream. His mouth was open, but nothing came out.

DJ Riggs sat, towel over his shoulders, cup of awful coffee in his hands. One of the narc cops who had caught him sat across from him. The other stood behind him.

DJ knew the drill. He knew the room. All these rooms and all these cops were the same. They had him. They could play back and forth, good cop, bad cop, we know what you did, do you know what's going to happen to you?, we don't need you to talk but it will go better for you if you do.

"You saved a baby," the cop across the table said. He was young, younger than DJ, Hispanic, long hair.

"That buy me a ticket out of here?" asked DJ.

"Not hardly," said the other narc behind him, a tall black man who looked like somebody on the Yankees DJ couldn't quite place. "But it inclines us to listen to anything you might have to tell us."

"Okay, I tell you I want a lawyer."

"We can't help you once your lawyer comes," said the Hispanic cop.

DJ looked at the wall. He could have been left alone and supplied all the dialogue.

"Yeah," he said. "And you want to help me."

"Hell of a thing you did saving that kid, coming out of that doorway so we could see you. Hell of a thing," said the Hispanic narc.

"We're inclined to be nice," said the black cop behind him.

"Okay," said DJ. "I've got something. Deal is, I give it to you and it's good shit, I walk."

"It would have to be damn good," said the first cop.

"It is," said DJ. "I want it on tape and I want to hear your voices on that tape and I want my lawyer to hear the deal."

"Deal is off the record," said the first cop. "You trust us or no deal. And there will be no deal anyway if you don't have some top quality information."

DJ looked at them and said, "I saved that baby's life."

"You did," agreed the black cop.

"Okay," said Riggs folding his arms. "Deal."

"Talk," said the black cop. "Make it good."

"Terrorist," said DJ.

Neither cop seemed moved by the information.

"I dealt him some detonators."

"You're a drug dealer," said the Hispanic cop.

"I'm an entrepreneur," said DJ.

"Go on," said the black cop.

"He came to me. Don't know how he knew I

was the man to come to. White guy, maybe fifty, one of those British accents, you know. I asked him if he needed bombs too. Not that I had them."

"Of course not," said the Hispanic cop. "More coffee?"

"No. All he wanted was detonators. I happened to know where I could get a few. Hoisted from a construction site over in Jersey."

"This man in search of detonators, he have a name?" asked the black cop.

"Everybody's got a name," said DJ, "but no one gives a real one to me and I'm fine with it."

"That's all you have?" asked the Hispanic cop.

"He made a cell phone call. He didn't know I could hear him. Argued with somebody, said whoever he was talking to should calm down, that everything would be fine, that he'd meet him at Doohan's in the morning."

"And when did this conversation happen?" asked the black cop.

"Last night," said DJ. "Did I give you enough?"

"We'll check your tale, talk to an assistant DA," said the Hispanic cop. "You can identify this British guy?"

"Damn straight," said DJ. "Am I walking?"

"You saved a baby," said the black cop.

"You dealt detonators to a possible terrorist," said the Hispanic cop. "Homeland Security will want to talk to you."

"And the FBI," said the black cop.

"Hey, man, I saved the baby."

"That you did," said the Hispanic cop. "It's in the mix." He looked up over DJ's shoulder and nodded. The door opened behind DJ and then closed.

"I want a lawyer now," said DJ.

"It's still raining hard," said the Hispanic cop.

"Then he'll just have to slog his way over here. I'm through talking," said DJ.

The Hispanic cop got up and motioned for DJ to do the same.

"How's the baby doin'?" asked DJ.

"High and dry. His mother's a crackhead. She lost track of him when she was high and the kid wandered off. Name's Linda Johnson. Know her?"

"Yeah," said DJ, thinking there was an outside chance that he had saved the life of his own baby.

7

IT NEVER RAINED like this in Poland.

Well, almost never.

Waclaw longed for a command of English. Instead his grasp of the language was more of a whimper. To be fair, Waclaw had been in the United States for less than two weeks and the lessons he had taken in Poland had proved to be almost useless.

He was on vacation from his job in Lodz. Actually, it was more of a pilgrimage than a vacation.

Waclaw wanted to see his son and daughter-in-law and their children before he died—if he indeed was going to die soon. He had a liver disease. There was a hospital in New York City where his son Alvin and his family lived, a hospital that specialized in liver disease. Waclaw had an appointment at

the hospital, but now the time of that appointment
had long passed.

The geography here eluded him. His son and his
family lived in Brooklyn. Brooklyn, he was told,
was part of the city. There were other parts of the
city, five of them, called boroughs. One of these
boroughs was the island he had heard of since he
was a boy, the island where his son worked, Manhattan. It was all very confusing to an outsider,
Waclaw thought.

Waclaw had an international driver's license.
His task had been simple: he would drive the five
blocks to the train station, park in the lot and wait
for his son to come home from work. Then his son
would drive them to the hospital.

Waclaw had not made it to the parking lot.

The rain had made driving so treacherous that
Waclaw had driven off the road. He saw a brown
patch of mud and water in front of him, lost control of the car and drove into what looked like
a river or a lake. The engine stopped. The lights
went out. The car surrendered to the rain, began
drifting out into the river.

Then Waclaw could feel the car sliding slowly
down farther into the water.

He tried to get out. The pressure of the water
and the angle at which he sat made it impossible
to open the door. His panic increased. But then the

car had stopped moving, with the water level at the bottom of the window.

And so there he had sat for four hours, according to his waterproof watch, while the rain pounded on the roof of the car and he fruitlessly scanned the shore for possible signs of help.

Waclaw was hungry. He was tired. He needed a shave. He probably needed a new liver.

The rain continued to fall.

Then he had an idea. He slowly opened the window. Water and rain blew in. Waclaw, who was lean and taut, eased his way through the window and took off his shoes, which would weigh him down. He looked toward the shore. He didn't think he could swim that far—he could barely swim at all—but he could float on his back. So that was what he did. Better that than sitting around and waiting for help that might never come. He eased into the rushing river, floating into darkness and a rain that tried to pelt him under.

Arthur Alexson was hunched over, head into the wind and rain. He had cut a hole in a large piece of clear plastic he had found in an empty furniture box. It made a fine poncho, though it whipped around hard and with a snap when the wind caught it. He had tied a length of frayed cord around the makeshift poncho the way he had seen

Sylvester Stallone do it in the first Rambo movie.

Arthur Alexson had a home, at least for now. The house he lived in was for sale. The people who owned it had moved somewhere. It was a nice house on a nice street with a basement window that didn't lock and which he entered after dark. He kept the finished basement clean and never went upstairs.

Arthur Alexson had left the house that morning, head and body bent over into the wind and rain in search of food. He had money, forty dollars, hard earned, asking for handouts right in front of the Fulton Street and Hoyt-Schermerhorn Street subway station entrances. It took him fifteen days to accumulate that much money, but what else did he have to do? He had spent five of his forty dollars for the goods he now hugged under the makeshift plastic poncho.

As he walked carefully along the muddy bank of the creek, Arthur noticed a spot of white drifting past him, heading for the East River. Arthur stopped. No doubt. It was a man, and the son-of-a-bitch was alive.

"I'll get you," called Arthur, as the pale man floating on his back flowed closer.

The man called back something in Chinese or Russian or some such shit.

Arthur ran ahead of the man, heading in the direction in which the man was floating. Slipping in the muddy embankment, almost sliding into the water, worrying about snakes, which he hated, Arthur searched until he found a broken tree branch. It wasn't much and it wasn't all that long, but it was that or watch that poor bastard float away.

Arthur very reluctantly put his plastic bag of food down after quickly tying the top. Then he held out the branch and shouted into the rain, "Over here. Here. Here."

Waclaw heard the voice and began to paddle awkwardly toward it even though he didn't understand the words. The waterway had narrowed, and Waclaw thought that even with his poor swimming skills he might be able to make it to the source of the voice.

"Come on. Come on. You can do it," called Arthur.

Waclaw neared the shore and felt something against his chest. It scratched and cut. He grabbed it and Arthur Alexson pulled him in and then grabbed his outstretched arms to drag Waclaw onto the embankment.

When he was sure the man was safe and wouldn't slip back in, Arthur sat and panted. He looked over his shoulder. His bag of groceries was still there.

"That was close," he said.

Waclaw, too exhausted to move, thanked him in Polish.

"You're welcome," said Arthur, shaking his head and taking off his poncho. He covered the man with it and said, "What's your name?"

Waclaw took his wallet out of his pants, reached into it and pulled out a card. Arthur looked at it.

"This is my father. His name is Waclaw and he does not speak English. My cell phone number is 1-888-000-CHEM."

The name printed at the bottom was Alvin Havel.

Mac pressed the top of the mouse and the screen of James Feldt's laptop appeared with a musical hum. The computer sat on Mac's desk next to a cup of hot herbal tea.

The tickle in his throat had become a discernible soreness. He didn't have to use a thermometer, but he knew that he had a temperature.

He knew that cold and flu viruses came from human-to-human transmission and were not caused by cold or damp weather. Mac had also concluded, with reservations, that cold and wet weather might well create conditions under which the cold virus was more easily transmitted.

In any case, Mac Taylor had a sore throat and a cold and maybe some kind of flu. He drank some of the lukewarm tea and examined the computer screen.

Columns of numbers faced him each with an

identification attached: "Woodrow Shelton, June Billing, $14,234; Monica Kobilski, June Billing, $18,333."

What interested Mac was the last entry on the page. It was a note that read:

> *Primary associate billing and carryover billing adjusted is %12.23 higher than adam

Adam. Lowercase. No period. Mac could imagine a number of ways to end the sentence including something like "higher than adam predicted." But this was the last thing Feldt had written. "adam." No time for capitalization?

The tea soothed for a few seconds. Mac took a bottle of aspirin from his desk, removed three tablets and downed them with the help of the tea. Then he popped a lemon lozenge into his mouth.

Mac pressed more keys and pulled up the photos of the two mutilation victims. He scanned the photos and found the ones that showed the letters *D* and *A* carved into the thighs of the victims.

Time of death. Of course. If it hadn't been for the semi-fog of the flu, he would have seen it earlier. The body of Patricia Mycrant had been found first, a *D* carved into her thigh. Then Feldt *A*. But the temperature and condition of the two bodies indicated that Feldt had been the first one murdered, which meant first *A* and then *D*. Adam?

Were there going to be four victims? Another *A* and then an *M*? Not enough evidence yet. He could be carving anything into the victims, perhaps his initials, A.D. Or the two letters were the beginning of another word they didn't yet know. It would take another corpse to confirm Mac's suspicion that the next letter would be another *A*.

The other corpse existed. And the second *A* was carved into his thigh. The mutilated dead man was Timothy Byrold. His body had just been discovered by Dorrie Clarke, who saw the partly open door to Timothy's apartment and pushed it open farther.

Dorrie had gone down the hall to retrieve a tennis ball she had thrown. Dorrie was six years old.

"Umbrella Man?" asked Flack.

"That's what he calls himself," said Achmed from behind the counter of the Brilliance Deli.

There were no customers. Those who had been there earlier to escape the downpour had all fled when the blood-red rain gushed through the awning. Most of them had hurried into the rain under umbrellas purchased from Dexter the Umbrella Man.

"No name?" Flack pressed. "The Umbrella Man?"

"Dexter," said Achmed.

"And he stepped out on the street?"

"As soon as the bloody rain started to flow

through the awning," Achmed said. "Went out there and looked up toward the roof, just stood there looking for a little while like he saw something or someone up there."

"How did he look?" asked Flack.

"Frightened, I think. Then he crossed the street and was gone."

Flack had stepped into the rain a few minutes earlier and looked up at the roof. Dexter the Umbrella Man would have been looking up at the spot where Mac had found evidence that the killer had leaned on the edge of the roof. Dexter the Umbrella Man could have seen the killer.

"And you don't know his last name or where he lives?" Flack asked Achmed.

"No, wait," said Achmed. "I know where he gets the umbrellas. He told me he gets the watches he sells when it isn't raining and the umbrellas when it is from somebody named Alberto, yes, at Alberto's place, I think he said on 101st Street."

"I know the place," said Flack.

His phone beeped.

"We've got another one," said Mac. "I'm on my way there. Find anything?"

"Maybe. Possible someone who saw the perp. And I want another crack at the victim's mother. Something's off about her. I feel it."

"Stay on it," Mac said. "Let me know if something turns up."

"Right," said Flack.

"You all right, Don?"

"Fine. Any news on Hawkes?"

"They're still working on it," Mac said. "I'll call you if I hear anything."

They hung up. Flack had a lot of ground to cover and the rain showed no sign of letting up.

Stella knelt next to the body of Henry Doohan, bartender and owner of what had been Doohan's Bar.

The gun that had killed Doohan had been fired at close range, very close. The entry wound and powder residue indicated to Stella that the gun had almost touched the right temple of the dead man's head. There was a large, rough-edged exit wound. Somewhere among the million or more remnants of the blast was a bullet or what remained of one. Stella would look for it. She might even find it.

She probed the dead man's nose with a swab and pried his mouth open to examine his tongue and throat. The swab would have to be examined microscopically. Stella examined the dead man's hands and took prints and scrapings from his palms. Then she covered the hands with plastic bags.

She was reasonably sure that Doohan had not shot himself. For one thing, there was no weapon near the body. For another, if she calculated the entry angle of the wound correctly, he would have had to hold the gun at an awkward angle and he would have to have been left-handed. The ME could insert a trajectory rod into the wound to confirm the angle of the wound. Doohan's watch was on his left wrist which more than strongly suggested that he was right-handed. That too could be confirmed.

Stella searched with flashlight and hands, reaching into nooks and puddles in search of the bullet. Nothing. She stood up and carefully made her way to the pit no more than two yards away where Hawkes and Custus were trapped. A lone young fireman knelt at the edge of the hole and monitored the pump that dropped down the sides of the pit and out of sight in the darkness.

"Hawkes," she called.

"Yes," Hawkes called back.

"Your cell phone working?"

"Wait . . . it's working."

"Answer it," she called, punching in his number.

Hawkes's fingers were growing numb. He kept flexing them and changing gloves to keep them warm. He flipped the phone open.

"Hear me?" Stella said.

"I hear," said Hawkes, looking at Custus who was gritting his teeth and grinning.

"What can we do besides keep working to get you out?"

"Morphine. He needs it."

"Morphine?" Stella said to the young fireman.

"I'll get Lieutenant Devlin," he said, rising and moving off.

"Hawkes, we ran the photos and samples back at the lab. Custus is a bomb maker."

"I'm not surprised," said Hawkes.

"IRA," she said. "At least he was. Left Ireland six years ago. The explosive he used to bring down this building was not up to standard IRA quality. This wasn't a terrorist bombing."

"What was it?" asked Hawkes.

"You might try asking Mr. Custus."

"I will," said Hawkes, looking at Custus, who was looking at him and listening. "Bonasera."

"Yes."

"I can hear a wall giving way down here."

"I'll see if I can get them to move a little faster."

"If they can't get us out right now," said Hawkes, "I've got to go in and get that bullet out. I think its pressing on the liver. If it penetrates the liver . . ."

"I get the picture," said Stella.

"Ironic," said Hawkes, looking at Custus. "I've got all the tools for removing a bullet from a dead body. Now I have a live one."

"Ironic," Stella agreed.

"There's more," he said. "I became a medical

examiner and now a field investigator because I didn't want to work on living people. I didn't want to have anyone's life in my hands again."

"I know," said Stella.

Devlin and the young fireman were back at the rim of the pit as Stella closed her phone.

Devlin showed her a blue plastic case that fit easily into his palm.

"Morphine. I'll get it down to him," said Devlin. "Let him know it's coming."

"What about . . . ?"

"I think we might have to take a chance or two here to get Doctor Hawkes and the other man out," said Devlin. "The sooner we can get down there, the better, before . . ."

"Before . . . ?" Stella asked.

"Before it collapses," he said. "I'm not overly concerned about it, but we're still better safe than sorry."

"You have a family?" Stella asked.

The other fireman had gone back to monitoring the pump.

"Mother, father, brother, sister," he said.

"Married?"

"No."

"I don't have any family," said Stella. "No mother, father, aunts, uncles, cousins, husbands or children."

"You can't go down," Devlin said. "I'm trained to

do it. I've done things like this before. You wouldn't know what to do."

"You could tell me," she said.

"We don't have the time and I don't think you'd have the strength that might be needed."

"I work out," she said.

"I bench-press three hundred and fifty pounds," he said. "This isn't a game of whose *cojones* are bigger, Detective."

"You're right," she said. "I'll get back to the dead. I know how to deal with them."

There was no answer at the number Alvin Havel had written on the card his father carried.

Maddie Woods, uniformed reception officer at the precinct, had tried the number four times before calling the telephone company and getting the address. A car was dispatched to check out the address before driving the shivering man there in the endless downpour.

There had been no problem finding dry clothes for the man to wear. There were three boxes of clothes in a closet next to the evidence room, clothes that had belonged to victims, drug dealers, a few murderers.

No one on duty spoke whatever it was Waclaw spoke. She did know the man's name, Waclaw Havel. That was all she could read on the international driver's license in his wallet. He had reluctantly given up the wallet after much coaxing as he dressed in a pair of brown oversize winter corduroy slacks and an XX large T-shirt with a pocket. On the back of the T-shirt were the words "Life Sucks."

Maddie, short and plump with dyed blonde hair in a feather cut, tried communicating with the wild-haired man by using creative sign language. She had one basic question. What the hell had happened to him and how did he get to the front door of the police station? Sign language proved fruitless. Officer Jimmy Tuskov was brought in from directing traffic. He tried Russian. Waclaw didn't understand. Jimmy tried Czech, of which he knew just enough to get by. No luck.

"It's Polish," Jimmy decided.

Detective Art Rogetti wandered by the room as Waclaw was speaking to Jimmy.

"What's he talkin'?" asked Art, who had a cup of coffee in his hand. Art was tall, thin with a little belly, and a year away from retirement.

"Polish," said Maddie with a sigh. "You talk Polish?"

"No," said Art. "But I know someone who does."

"Who's that?" asked Maddie.

"Perp I'm bringing this coffee to," said Art. "Caught him looting a porno shop."

"It's not being called looting yet," said Jimmy.

"Okay. B and E then," said Art. "You want the guy?" he asked Maggie. "You don't want the guy?"

"We want the guy," said Maddie.

"Good, then I'll get the guy. His name is Zbilski."

A few seconds later a tough-looking little man in his late twenties was marched sullenly into the room. He looked at Waclaw and said something in Polish. Waclaw answered eagerly.

"What do I get?" asked Zbilski.

"Our sincere thanks," said Art.

"I just forgot how to speak Polish," said Alex.

"Remember fast," said Art. He handed the coffee to Zbilski.

Waclaw looked at Zbilski and said, "Rozumiesz polsku?" (Do you understand Polish?)

Zbilski answered, "Mowie po polsku."

"Well?" asked Art.

"Maybe it's coming back to me," said Zbilski.

"You deliver, you walk," said Art. "I'm feeling generous and curious." Truth was, Art didn't have enough evidence on Zbilski to be sure the breaking and entering charge would stick anyway.

After five minutes of talking to Zbilski, the three police officers knew why Waclaw had found his way to the station.

"Havel," Art said, looking at the driver's license Maddie had handed him. "Name rings bells. Wait a second."

Art left the room. Waclaw spoke again.

"He wants to know what happened to the car," said Zbilski.

"What car?" asked Maddie. "We've got abandoned cars all over the place."

Waclaw was in the process of explaining when Art returned and said, "Ask him if his son is Alvin Havel, the school teacher."

Zbilski asked. Waclaw said yes.

"He's dead," said Art. "Murdered at the school in Manhattan where he teaches."

"You want me to tell him?" asked Zbilski.

The three police officers exchanged looks.

"Make it gentle," said Maddie. "Real gentle and you walk. Okay with you, Art?"

Art nodded his agreement. Jimmy shrugged.

Zbilski smiled and handed the coffee he was holding to Waclaw, who accepted it with two hands. Then Zbilski leaned over, hand on the older man's shoulder and told him, gently.

Waclaw took a sip of coffee and handed the cup back to Zbilski, who handed it to Art. Then Waclaw wept and rocked and started to talk rapidly.

"What's he saying?" asked Jimmy.

"He's talking too fast," said Zbilski, who asked Waclaw in Polish to slow down.

Waclaw looked at him and kept talking.

"He says he knows who killed his son," said Zbilski. "He knows who and he knows why. He told his son to stop, but his son wouldn't listen. Now he's dead. His only son."

"Who does he think killed his son?" Maddie asked.

Zbilski asked the question and Waclaw Havel answered.

"What'd he say?" asked Maddie.

"He said, 'She did it,'" said Zbilski.

"Who is she?" asked Tuskow.

Zbilski asked and Waclaw answered.

"She's in the book," Zbilski translated.

"The book?" asked Art. "The phone book?"

Waclaw spoke rapidly. Zbilski said, "Wow wolniej."

Zbilski looked at the cops as Waclaw began speaking and said, "I asked him to slow down. Just says 'the book,'" said Zbilski.

"Che mi sie siusiu," said Waclaw.

"What'd he say?" asked Maddie.

"He has to pee," said Zbilski.

8

CONNOR DRANK HIS DRAFT BEER *and smiled at the foam.*

What had he come to? Sitting in the middle of the morning nursing a beer in a First Avenue bar while he waited for a frightened jack rabbit to come skulking in. The man he was waiting for would have to be urged, nudged, wheedled into what Connor planned, but he was reasonably sure he could do it. Connor had done his homework.

Once, both long ago and not that long ago, Connor had commanded respect. He was a bloody bombing genius, first for the IRA and then for anyone who would pay for his expertise and daring. But fewer and fewer wanted his artistry. There were bombers and bomb makers all over the globe blowing everything up, including themselves. And these amateurs were called masterminds. There had been a time when if a group with a grievance had wanted something blown up, Connor was their boy. Only Connor hadn't been a boy for a long time and he'd had to fall back on his other profession, which paid him only slightly better in the long run than explosives.

Now he sat at a bar on a rainy morning, the only customer in a bar that still smelled of cigars, cigarettes and burnt burgers from the night before.

The Wheel and Wagon pub back home had always smelled of wax and whiskey and good beer and stout in the morning. At The Wheel, you could always expect to see someone you knew, not to mention the occasional visit by the police. Connor knew the police. Some of them even sat down with Connor to drink a pint and talk about how they were going to put Connor away again someday, put him away for good.

They never had, although he had almost put himself away two or three times. Had he stayed back home and nursed drinks and searched for new tales to tell at The Wheel, he could have counted on a relatively long life. But there was no longer a living to be made in Dublin. So Connor had packed one night and left a note for his brother. And he was gone.

Connor could have made a good living working for terrorists who seemed to be everywhere but the North and South Poles. And they would, he had no doubt, be up and down there too when the ice caps melted and the polar bears roamed down to Kansas. But Connor would not work for crazy people, and terrorists were crazy people. You couldn't trust crazy people with crazy eyes who didn't care who they killed. In Connor's book, you warned and cleared before you blew a place up. If you happened to kill, you regretted it and said a prayer for the dead and your own soul and a "God Bless Ireland." Then you put it aside. Nothing you could do about it when it was done. You put it aside and engaged in banter with friends old and new and acquaintances.

"Another?"

The bartender, a young man with a dark look that said he had known what it was like behind other bars, stood near him.

"Why not?" said Connor.

The bartender nodded and moved off to get a second beer for his only customer on a less than promising morning.

Reduced, Connor thought. Reduced to haggling with a drug dealer named DJ Riggs for a handful of detonators and an Afghan fence named Hamid for a half dozen sticks of badly stored and wrapped dynamite.

The door opened behind Connor. He heard the rain beating down behind whoever had entered. He felt a slight whoosh of warm wind on his back. The door closed. Connor didn't turn. The bartender placed a fresh mug before him. The foam waterfalled out and down the rim and Connor drank.

Someone sat next to him. He could smell the musk of

rain on the man, but he did not look. There was a role to play. Connor had played it many times before.

"Are you . . . ?" the man at his side said.

"That depends," said Connor, "on who you're looking for. Since I'm the only one in here besides the dapper barkeep, it's likely I'm the one you seek."

With that Connor turned his head and looked at the man at his side. The man was wet and shivering, though the rain was warm. The man was about Connor's age but he was lean, wore an ill-fitting toupee and lacked fortitude.

"I just want to be sure," the man said, looking at the bartender who was on the phone, his back turned.

"The name to conjure by is Terrence Williams," said Connor. "Though I doubt if that's his real name. He's less a Terrence than a Slobodon. You agree with that assessment?"

"I don't know," said the man who bore a look that told Connor he was wondering what he had gotten into. "It's got to look like an accident."

"I know my business," said Connor, suddenly serious and sober. "Twenty-five thousand plus expenses."

"Expenses?"

Connor shook his head and said, "My room and board and the means of making and putting into effect the device. And how do I know this isn't some kind of trap, a sting? That figures into the expense, the risk factor. You need to make it clearer, show me evidence that you are who you say you are."

The man grappled for his wallet. It was working. Connor had taken the initiative, questioned the mark before the mark could question him. The bartender approached.

"My friend will have the same," Connor said, tapping his mug.

The bartender nodded and walked away.

The man finally wrestled the wallet out of his pocket.

Connor took it from his hand and opened it. Driver's license. Credit cards. Automobile insurance card. Blue Cross Blue Shield card. Savings and loan card. Eighty-four dollars and a tarnished Susan B. Anthony dollar coin tucked behind a library card.

Connor held up the coin.

"Good luck?"

"I don't know. I just carry it."

Connor handed the coin and wallet back to the man.

"How do we—?"

"How do I," Connor corrected. "I've looked at the place. Not a great challenge. Half the money plus three thousand for expenses upfront. The rest when the festivities are over."

"Cash?"

Connor put a hand on the man's shoulder and said, "What am I going to do with a bloody check?"

"I'll make it out to cash."

"And I'll have to endorse it. Stop the shuffle and come up with the cash or we part our ways and say no more, much to the loss of both vendor and vendee."

"When will you do it?"

"No point in waiting for the full moon or a bright sun," said Connor. *"The rain looks as if it will be with us for a while. Two days?"*

"Two days," the man repeated. *"Yes."*

"I think I'll sit right here, dry and in the good company of our loquacious innkeeper while you round up the cash and return."

"How do I know—?"

"My reputation," said Connor, leaning into the man's face, his voice menacing. *"My pride. You sense them?"*

"Yes," said the man.

"Good," said Connor, sitting back, smiling and clapping his hands together. *"Now if you would go out into this gray and wet day and return with my payment, I'll buy you a drink."*

"I don't drink," the man said. *"I'm a bartender, remember?"*

"There's a law in the colonies against bartenders drinking? I wonder what the vintner drinks that's half so good as what he sells. Omar Khayyam or thereabouts."

"I have a liver disease," said the man.

"Well-earned by a dissolute life, I hope?" said Connor.

"No, a blood transfusion."

"No offense, dear patron, but you are beginning to depress me. Into the dark and damp day with you."

The man got off the stool, paused for a second or two, clearly wondering if he should or could change his mind.

"Indecision is a bore," said Connor. "Solace is a beer."

The man left.

"You got something a man can eat? Something that won't kill him?" Connor asked the bartender.

"Ham sandwich," said the bartender. "Bread's fresh."

"One of those with mustard," said Connor. "And some pretzels or salted nuts would be welcome."

The bartender nodded.

The job promised to be quick and easy. No one hurt. Pack up. Collect the rest of the payment. Head for JFK with a ticket for Toronto. And then to Australia to wait for the really big payoff.

Connor smiled and promised he would take care of the pesky tooth on the bottom in the back that had plagued him for months.

Quick and easy. Only it wouldn't be quick and easy.

It would go wrong, decidedly, disastrously, deadly wrong.

Two Months Earlier
Manhattan

It wasn't reasonable to expect a normal man with normal impulses to ignore them, the girls. They knew. He knew. It wasn't a matter of self control.

Alvin Havel had, for five years, pretended that the girls, their hair washed and shimmering, their breasts bobbing, their faces clean and clear and their legs . . .

Alvin had pretended, had worked hard at being a good teacher, making chemistry interesting, fun. He had succeeded.

The students, rich and confident, or pretending to be, talked of homes in the city and in Vermont or Connecticut or the Bahamas where they had their own Lexus or BMW or Mercedes. They talked of trips to Paris or Tokyo or Sydney.

Summers were supposed to be recovery time for teachers, a perk for having chosen a profession that precluded a decent mortgage. Alvin spent his summers teaching. If the students didn't want to be in school during the academic year, they wanted to be there even less in the summer. Summer school was punishment. Sullen faces, arms folded across chests, drowsy eyes. And the girls. The summer didn't give him a break. He had to see them hot and tanned.

Most of them were smart. Some of them were brilliant. A few of them were interested in chemistry.

The morning had been frost layered, a crisp chill. Then the school had been too warm, the heat turned up. Staying awake for students and teachers was a challenge.

He had given them a quiz. It was too warm in the room to think of real teaching. A quiz would keep them busy for twenty minutes. Then they'd discuss the quiz and class would be over.

She had come up to him with a question. The other students watched without looking. She had whispered her question, her mouth almost touching his ear. He could smell her hair. Her blue silk blouse was unbuttoned at the top and he had nowhere to look but at her breasts.

He answered her question and asked her if he could see her after class. He had a free period. She had lunch. She said yes.

After class when the others were gone, she stood in front of his desk, head cocked to one side, a knowing smile on her lips.

Alvin closed the classroom door and faced her. He tried to hide his trembling.

"Am I in trouble?" she asked.

"No," he said, knowing that what he was about to do, if he was not careful, could ruin his life.

"Then what?" she asked.

"I'd like your help," he said.

"My help?"

He walked toward her, a pensive look on his face.

"An experiment I'd like to conduct. If it works out, I want to write a paper."

"Publish or perish," she said as he moved in front of her.

"Yes," he said.

She took a step back as he moved forward.

"And what do you want me to do?" she asked.

"I've got to balance six different elements. I need someone coordinated to keep track of each element, see that nothing is going wrong."

He was looking into her eyes. She met his gaze.

"Let me see your hands," he said.

"My hands?"

"Hands, fingers," he said. "I want to be sure they're clean enough for the job."

The look on her face was a combination of skepticism and amusement. She held out a hand. God, she looked beautiful. What the hell was he doing?

He took her hand and ran his thumb along the palm.

"Good," he said. "Very good."

She smiled. It was midmorning. He was flirting. She was amused. Mr. Havel was cute. Mr. Havel was safe.

"Are you interested?" he asked.

His mouth was dry.

"Interested?"

"In the experiment."

"I don't know," she said. "I don't have much time."

"You think about it," he said. "If you like, you can take a look at what I've assembled so far. It might help you make up your mind."

She shrugged.

"Back in the storeroom," he said, guiding her to the back of the classroom.

He slid the white board over and stepped behind her into the room.

This was crazy. He should stop. Not too late. In a few minutes, no, a few seconds, he could have a screaming girl in front of him. His life, his career, could be over.

"Where?" she asked when he turned on the light.

He touched her shoulder. She turned to face him. He closed the sliding door.

She wasn't afraid. She was interested, curious. A kiss in the closet. A teacher who would owe her. She didn't intend to use it against him, but it would be fun just knowing she could and knowing that he knew.

He kissed her. He smelled her hair, felt her breasts against his chest. Her mouth was open.

And as she pulled back gently with both hands on his chest, she thought that would be the end of it. She touched his cheek and reached for the door.

Alvin grabbed her arm, turned her and kissed her again. This time she didn't respond. She didn't fight him, but she didn't respond.

Then he put a hand under her blouse and she said, "Hey, no."

He pushed her back against the wall. He didn't care what would happen. Wrong and right didn't matter. He whispered, "No one can hear. I want you to enjoy it. I don't want to hurt you."

She was afraid now, very afraid. He was bigger than she was, stronger than she would have guessed and he looked crazy, no longer the smiling, helpful, funny Mr. Havel.

She didn't fight. She didn't want to make him angry. All she wanted was to get out of there. It wasn't as if she were a virgin. She told herself that made a difference, *didn't really believe it. She thought about water, waves, imagined the sound of waves against the shore. She just wanted it to be over.*

And when it was he got off of her and said, "Are you all right?"

The Mr. Havel she knew had returned.

He helped her up. She didn't answer. She didn't look at him. The unasked question was in the air. Would she tell? She decided that she wouldn't give him the answer.

He would have to wait and suffer. If she wanted to, she could go into the hall now, screaming, sobbing, but she didn't. She knew she couldn't wait long. She adjusted her skirt and blouse. She started to sob and tried to stop, not wanting him to see her weakness.

"I'm sorry," he said. "I couldn't . . ."

She slid the storeroom door open and stepped into the classroom. Alvin stepped out behind her.

"Are you . . . ?" he began, but she had gathered her books and, biting her lower lip, hurried to the classroom door and then out into the corridor alive with students moving, talking, laughing, having no idea of what had happened.

She did not look back at Alvin Havel. She was already planning.

She would kill him. Not today. Not this week. He had to suffer, had to be afraid every time he looked at her.

She would kill him. She might need help. She knew where to get it.

She would kill him. She didn't have to expose herself,

*be humiliated by police, by probing hospital hands. She
wouldn't have to deal with her parents' anger and an-
guish.*

She would kill him. And two months later she did.

Two Years Earlier
Hempstead, Long Island

*Adam was ashamed. Adam was afraid. Adam did not
want to go to the pet shop where he worked after school
and on Saturdays. Adam loved animals. He had been
grateful when his father's old friend Larry Beckerman
had offered him the job. He wasn't grateful anymore.*

*Three weeks ago, after Adam had been working at the
pet shop for two months, Mr. Beckerman had told him he
needed help in the storeroom. A new shipment of cages
had come in and had to be priced, labeled and put on
shelves. It was a slow Tuesday night.*

*Adam was a small fifteen-year-old. Larry Beckerman
was a tall, broad, muscular forty-eight-year-old father of
three boys.*

*It began with Beckerman touching Adam's hand as
he held up a cage to be labeled. Minutes later, when he
was lifting a large cage, Beckerman reached over Adam's
shoulder and ran a hand down his chest before reaching
out to help with the cage.*

*Then, when Adam was washing his hands in the
small washroom next to the storeroom, Beckerman came
in, started to reach for a towel past Adam's face and*

*then suddenly grabbed, both arms around Adam's chest.
Adam tried to get away.*

*"It's going to happen no matter what you do," Becker-
man whispered. "I won't hurt you."*

*Beckerman had kissed his neck. Adam smelled some-
thing on Beckerman's breath that might have been that
morning's breakfast bacon.*

*"Don't scream," Beckerman said. "No one can hear
you."*

*The caged animals chattered, mewed, crackled, cried
and barked.*

*One of Beckerman's sons, Nick, was Adam's age. They
had classes together, but they weren't friends. Nick was a
jock like his two brothers. Adam wasn't quite a nerd, but
he wasn't varsity material.*

*"Tell anyone about this and I call you a liar," said
Beckerman. "I don't plan on doing anything that will
leave evidence. Take it easy. Enjoy it."*

*Beckerman's hand slipped down between Adam's legs.
Adam, through his fear and hyperventilation, felt something stir. And that was the beginning. He was drenched
in sweat, fear and shame.*

*When it was over, Adam knew he couldn't tell any-
one what Beckerman had done to him and what he had
been forced to do to Beckerman, an old family friend, his
father's college roommate.*

*Adam could have quit the pet shop, could have said
he had too much schoolwork to do, that he was afraid his
grades would drop. He could have, but Beckerman told*

him he had better not. He could have told his parents, written to his brother, told the police. But what if they believed him? Everyone would know what he had done to Beckerman. He would be be Adam the Queer, Adam the Queen. He would hear it, would know it by how everyone looked at him even if they didn't say it.

He took solace in the animals, the puppies and kittens, the cockatoo who said, "So's your old man," "Hold your horses," and "GI Jive."

And dutifully, maybe once a week—he never knew when it would happen—Beckerman would call him into the storeroom. Saturdays were safe from Beckerman. Too busy. But weekdays were different.

And then, one Tuesday, summoned to the storeroom, told to get on his knees, Adam took hold of Beckerman's hand and bit, bit hard as Beckerman, pants down around his ankles, struggled to keep from falling, screaming in sudden agony.

Adam tasted blood. Beckerman tripped.

"No more," Adam said.

"Get out," Beckerman had answered, lying on his back, his head resting against a small burlap sack of birdseed.

Adam had left. He told no one. Said he had quit. He dreaded the possibility of seeing Beckerman again, or anyone in Beckerman's family. But it was more than a possibility. Beckerman and Adam's father remained friends. Beckerman said he had been bitten by the cockatoo.

Adam grew quiet, too quiet, and distant. His par-

ents were concerned. They said they wanted him to see a counselor. He said he was fine and made an effort to look and act fine. The effort was draining, the memories overwhelming.

Four weeks after he had bitten the hand that abused him, Adam wrote a letter to his brother. He could have emailed, but the email would have existed in cyberspace forever. He asked his brother to destroy the letter after he read it. Adam apologized for writing the letter, but he had to tell someone.

A month after he mailed the letter there was still no answer. One night Adam said good night to his mother and father, straightened his bookcases, cleaned up the clutter in his room, and made sure the blanket on his bed was neat and unwrinkled. Then he showered, put on a clean shirt, underwear and pants and hanged himself from a crossbeam in his room.

9

THE FOUND AGAIN SHOP on Ninth Avenue was a block away from a successful off-Broadway theater that specialized in small musicals.

The shop wasn't nearly as upscale as Gladys Mycrant had suggested, although it certainly wasn't a standard resale shop. A sign in the window read: *Wear Today What the Famous Wore Yesterday for 1/10th the cost.*

There was only one customer, a young woman with an umbrella, who zipped through racks of clothing with a screech of hangers. Gladys had been standing at the back of the shop next to three tall mirrors. She was speaking to another woman, about Gladys's age, who also looked like a salesperson.

When Gladys saw Don Flack, she stopped talking, folded her arms and watched him approach.

"Doesn't look like you're too busy," said Flack. "Maybe we can talk now."

The other woman, dark, Mediterranean, Italian, Greek? looked puzzled.

"He's a policeman," Gladys explained. "My daughter was murdered this morning."

The other woman's mouth opened.

"I'd better talk to him."

"Yes. Yes. I'm . . ." the other woman stammered.

"It's fine," said Gladys. "Please."

Myra headed off in the direction of the lone customer.

"Mrs. Mycrant—"

"Gladys, if you are going to be polite and pleasant. Mrs. Mycrant, if you plan to be officious and threatening."

"Polite and pleasant," Flack said.

"Good."

"We don't know anything about your daughter," he said. "We don't know why anyone would want to kill her."

"I suppose it can't be a random killing," she said.

"Not during a rainstorm on the roof of your apartment building after she got a phone call and hurried out."

"No, not likely is it?"

"What can you tell me about her?"

"Patricia was smart, willful and hardworking when she had something to work hard at," Gladys said, meeting his eyes.

"She must have had some friends, people she knew, things she was interested in," he tried.

"She wasn't allowed to meet with the few people she knew."

"Wasn't allowed?"

"It was a condition of her parole," said Gladys. "My daughter was a convicted sexual predator, as you no doubt know."

"He walked funny. Like this," Dorrie said, demonstrating how the limping man had looked.

She had seen him coming down the corridor.

"He smiled at me like this," she told Mac, showing a sad smile.

"Was he young? Old?"

"Old like you mostly," she said.

They were sitting on the steps to the second floor. Dorrie was alone for the day with her ball, her toys, the television.

There was no school today. Her mother was working at Jack the Steamer's, six blocks away. Jack the Steamer operated one of a few dozen illegal shops that prepared meat products—hot dogs, gyros, souvlaki—for illegal pushcarts.

Jack the Steamer operated out of the back of

Wargo's Electronics. Today the carts were not coming by. Even the most desperate pushcart men who had families to feed and no green card for other work couldn't see the point in getting swept away. Besides, who would buy knishes in a deluge?

When the uniformed cop named Kovich who knew the neighborhood had come through the door, Jack the Steamer was sure that this was the final nail in his palm on the worst day of his life. Kovich, however, was not there to make a bust or get a free fake kosher red hot. He had come to fetch Dorrie's mother, Rena Prince.

In the apartment building where Mac and Dorrie sat six blocks away, a voice boomed down from above, a man's voice, vigorously arguing in a language Mac didn't understand.

"That's Laird," Dorrie explained. "He's crazy. He makes up his own words."

"He talk to himself like that a lot?" asked Mac.

"A lot."

"Did he do it this morning before you found . . . ?"

"Yes. He doesn't hurt anybody. When he comes out of his apartment, he's very sad, very nice."

"Sad like the limping man?"

"Yes."

"You know anyone really old, older than me and the limping man?"

"Oh yeah. Jack. He's a nice guy. When I go to

work with my mom, he gives me stuff to eat. You want to know a secret?"

"Sure," said Mac.

"I think it smells bad at Jack's and the food tastes like shit."

With that Officer Kovich and Rena Prince appeared.

The woman was no more than twenty-five, skinny, pale, smooth, pretty face with hair held in place by a rubber band.

"I don't leave Dorrie alone," she said, moving in front of her daughter and taking her hand. "Do I, Dore?"

"Nope. Just when school gets closed and you can't get me to Tanya's in Brooklyn."

"Officer," Mac said. "Mind taking Dorrie back to her apartment?"

"Sure thing," said Kruger. "Come on, Dorrie."

He held out his hand. She shook her head "no" to the hand but followed the officer down the hall.

"We're not here to arrest you for neglect," Mac said when they were out of earshot. "Timothy Byrold in One-A was murdered a few hours ago. Dorrie found the body."

"Oh," said Rena. "I've got to—"

"This will just take a few seconds," Mac said gently.

"Was it—?" she began and halted.

"It wasn't good," said Mac. "Dorrie seems to be handling it pretty well."

"She's seen too much. A kid shouldn't see what she's seen."

Mac had a feeling the woman was talking not just about what her daughter had seen, but what she herself had seen and experienced.

"You know Mr. Byrold?"

"A little. Dorrie talked to him more than I did. Seemed harmless, but who the hell really knows, you know?"

Mac nodded. "He have any friends, visitors?"

"He lives in that apartment. I mean, lived there. Once a week, Wednesday's I think, he went to some meeting downtown. No visitors. Well, I did see some guy knocking at his door about a month ago when I was going to work."

"What did this guy look like?"

"Nice looking. Maybe thirty. Clean slacks, nice pullover. Built like he worked out."

"You got a good look?"

"Yeah. I thought he might say hello. I don't see many good-looking, clean guys in my life."

She looked around the hall as if to illustrate the boundaries of her existence.

"Byrold let him in?"

"Yes. He knocked. Tim said, 'Who is it.' He said . . . Don? Dom? Who remembers?"

"Only visitor?"

"Only one I ever saw. Tim opened the door. Guy limped in."

"Limped?"

"Yeah, I figured he hurt his leg or something."

"And you could recognize him again if you saw him?"

"Oh, yes," she said. "You think he killed Tim?"

Mac didn't answer.

Above them Laird the Loud shouted in gibberish and then let out a triumphant laugh. Rena looked up the stairs and then at Mac.

"Welcome to our life," she said. "Can I go be with my baby now?"

"Go ahead," said Mac.

The mutilated corpse of Timothy Byrold was definitely the work of the same person who had killed Patricia Mycrant and James Feldt.

Before Mac had checked for prints or examined the body for strands of hair that didn't belong; before he had taken samples of blood or scraped under the dead man's fingernails; Mac had used a swatch of gauze dipped in alcohol to clear away just enough blood to read the letter *A* carved into Timothy Byrold's thigh.

Mac was not surprised. They had found Patricia Mycrant first, *D*. Then James Feldt, *A*, and now Timothy Byrold, another *A*. *DAA*. But that was not the timeline of the murders, just the order in which they had found the bodies. The actual sequence was *ADA*. The name Feldt had typed onto his computer was "adam." Rena Prince had seen a limping man go into Byrold's apartment. The man had identified himself as "Don" or "Dom." Could it have been "Adam"?

The killer with a limp was not finished. It was only three in the afternoon. Plenty of time left in the day and who could be certain that he would be finished when he had finished spelling Adam? Perhaps there was a last name too.

Maybe Sid Hammerbeck could come up with something more.

After he had talked to Dorrie and her mother, Mac's cell phone rang. It was Leonard Giles.

"You going to be back here in the reasonable future?"

"On my way," said Mac.

"Good. Something interesting on the Stanwick Oil building security tapes from this morning."

"A limping man," said Mac.

"A limping man," said Giles. "I assume that was no prescient guess."

"No."

"No clear view of his face," said Giles. "Hooded. Guard doesn't know how the man with the limp got past him. Guard is seventy, wears significant glasses and requires frequent visits to the bathroom."

"Thanks," said Mac.

"You haven't heard it all," said Giles. "I played some computer games, videos from rehab centers of people with permanent leg trauma."

"The limp," said Mac.

"The limp," Giles agreed. "I looked at and did overlays of the videos and those of the man in the lobby."

"And you found?"

"Our limping man has an artificial leg," said Giles.

"You're sure?"

"I am acutely aware of the various causes of crippling trauma. An artificial leg is an awkward thing to hide, but it can be done with a great deal of patience and practice. All of which suggests that our limping man suffered his loss in the past year or so. He's still learning."

"I'm on my way," said Mac. "Thanks."

Mac picked up his kit and headed down the hallway, the ranting Laird's voice bellowing above. His phone rang again. "Yeah."

"Mac. What've you got?"

"Another corpse," he told Flack. "A suspect. You?"

"Something very interesting about Patricia Mycrant, a possible motive for her murder. And more."

Flack told Mac what he had learned from Gladys Mycrant.

"Follow it," Mac said.

"I will," said Flack. "You inside or out?"

"In, going out."

"Surprise waiting for you on the street," said Flack. "The rain stopped."

"So what have we got?" Danny asked, looking at the computer screen.

The head and neck of a man with a rod sticking out of his neck and another protruding from his eye almost filled the screen. Danny worked the mouse and the head began to slowly turn. He worked the mouse again and the rods turned red. The depth of the intrusion of the rods was clearly visible.

"Neck wound, the one that killed him, the first blow, is at a thirty-degree angle from back to front," said Danny. "Conclusion?"

Lindsay made a fist with her right hand and reached over. She made a thrust toward Danny's neck.

"If the killer was right-handed," she said, "and struck from in front of the victim, he—"

"Or she," added Danny.

"Or she," Lindsay agreed, "was pretty strong. Wound is three inches deep through flesh and bone."

"And with a pencil," said Danny.

"Strong killer."

"And Havel just stood there."

"He didn't expect it," said Lindsay.

"So if he's sitting or standing behind his desk and someone comes out of the closet and starts coming at him with a sharp pencil in his hand . . ."

"He's not just going to stand there quietly waiting and then let himself be stabbed," she said.

"With a pencil," said Danny, shaking his head. "Why didn't the killer use a knife, or one of the metal rods in the closet?"

"I don't know," said Lindsay. "Unless he didn't plan to kill Havel. He came at him, got angry, picked up a pencil from the desk and—"

"What if the killer was left-handed?" asked Danny.

"Look at the angle," she said. "The blow would have to have been struck from behind and the thrust . . ."

She demonstrated.

"Would have to have been forward."

Danny manipulated the image of the head toward him. The rod in the neck slowly pulled out. The head turned away. The rod went back in with a jolt.

"He'd have to have been standing," said Danny. "Or the killer had to have been kneeling behind him."

"Not likely," said Lindsay.

"Not likely," Danny agreed. "But what about the other blow, the pencil in the eye?"

"After Havel was dead," Lindsay said. "What sense does that make?"

Danny touched the keys on the pad in front of him and the rod slowly pulled out of the eye.

"No angle," he said. "Straight in, almost four inches. It looks as if it were pounded in with a hammer."

"Not a hammer," Lindsay said, "but something. The eraser is almost torn off."

She reached past Danny, hit some keys and a report appeared on the screen. He read it slowly. "Traces of glass."

He sat back, put his hands behind his head and looked at her.

"How'd you like to take a trip back to school, Montana? See what we may have missed?"

"Why not?"

"The rain's stopped," he said. "Want to pick up a couple of coffees on the way?"

"Why not," she said again. "And let's call Stella, see how Hawkes is doing."

"The rain stopped," Hawkes said.

"But the sky is still falling," answered Custus, his eyes closed.

And he was right.

Hawkes held the bullet he had removed from Custus's side. He dropped it in an evidence bag and placed the bag in his kit.

"How are you feeling?" asked Hawkes.

Custus laughed, choked on his laughter, coughed and finally grew calm enough to say, "Perfect. You just removed a bullet from me in less than anti-septic circumstances. My ankle is pinned under a beam and broken. Water is rising, which is likely to drown me before I'm killed by infection. I hope you're not going to suggest amputating my leg to get me out of here. I'd prefer a quiet morphine-lulled departure from this earth."

"I'm not going to cut off your leg," Hawkes said.

"Good. Do I gather that you just surgically saved my life?"

"I think so," said Hawkes. "At least the threat isn't there anymore."

"Not from the bullet, anyway."

"You want to tell me how you got shot?"

"I think not," said Custus. "It's all quite unclear to me."

Hawkes could hear what sounded like a wooden beam cracking coming from the deep darkness.

The end of the rain didn't mean the end of the water flowing into the pit. It was now a de-ceptively soothing waterfall working against the pump, which barely kept up with the flow.

"Might as well try to get yourself out of here, Doc," Custus said. "That's not to say I want you to stop trying to get me out too, but what's the point of your sharing my fate if it comes to that.

I've been arms-around-the-neck with death more times than a buck in hunting season. It makes for the illusion of having lived a long eventful life."

"You threw the gun away," said Hawkes.

"That I did."

"I saw where you threw it," said Hawkes.

Custus let out a choking laugh.

"And you're going to try to retrieve it? I take back my suggestion that you try to get the hell out of here. If you're going to act like a fool, you can die like one kneeling at the side of an even bigger fool."

Hawkes pulled a pill bottle from his kit, poured three pills into his palm and said, "Open your mouth."

"I haven't had it closed since we started to share this little grotto."

Custus opened his mouth, accepted the pills and swallowed them.

"Thanks," he said.

Hawkes got to his feet in a crouch and, flashlight in hand, moved into the darkness.

"You're really going to do it," marveled Custus. "I've known many a fool and flirted with the appellation myself on more than one occasion, but you are about to take the trophy and hold it for life, which, in your case, does not promise to be long."

To punctuate the prediction, the beam in the darkness let out a jagged scream.

Hawkes froze for an instant and then was gone. Custus tried to turn his head to see him but he was pinned too firmly.

"Hawkes," a woman called above Custus.

"He's occupied," croaked Custus.

"I know what happened," said Stella.

Custus couldn't see her, but he could tell from her voice what she probably meant.

"May I suggest that you get someone down here to pull that stubborn physician out. You might need a strait jacket since he seems to be enamored of both my company and our new accommodations."

"The firemen are working on it," she said.

"They'd best work quickly or their work will be done all too soon," said Custus. "I've grown fond of Doctor Hawkes."

"I'm glad," said Stella.

"A question."

"Yes," called Stella, leaning as close to the pit as she could.

"Are you beautiful?"

"Ravishing," said Stella. "You?"

"I am not beautiful," said Custus. "I'm a wasted husk with a broken ankle and a hole in my side, but in my day, which was as recent as last week, I was considered quite intriguing to the ladies."

"You blew up this building," Stella said.

Custus didn't answer.

"Four people died in the explosion."

Custus still didn't answer.

"Another one was shot before the explosion," she said.

"I plead semi-innocent of all accusations," said Custus. "If I survive, I'll gladly do the right thing. I'll suddenly stop talking."

"You shot Doohan," said Stella.

Hawkes appeared, gun in hand, and knelt next to Custus just as the beam gave a deep sigh of defeat and gave way. The walls and ceiling came down with a crash. The water level rose in a gush and a gray-white dust filled the air and pushed into Hawkes's nose and mouth.

Hawkes leaned over in an attempt to protect Custus's face.

The cracking and crumbling diminished but didn't stop.

Hawkes could see that the space in the pit in which he and Custus sat had now been reduced to about the size of the backseat of a midsize car.

"His name is Adam," said Mac. "He walks with a limp, has an artificial leg."

He and Flack were seated in chairs across the desk from Paul Sunderland, psychologist. Sunderland was white teethed, athletically built, and only his slightly gray close-cropped hair suggested that he was over forty.

The usual degrees were mounted on the wall near the door where they couldn't be missed. The photos on the other walls were of Sunderland in shorts and helmet, with one hand on a bicycle that, Flack was sure, had to cost more than a thousand dollars.

Sunderland had a small blue ball in his hand. He kept squeezing the ball and from time to time switched hands.

"Yeah," said Sunderland. "I know him. Adam Yunkin."

"How about Patricia Mycrant, James Feldt, Timothy Byrold?" asked Flack.

Sunderland hesitated and looked at the two detectives.

"Patricia Mycrant's mother told us she was seeing you," said Flack.

Sunderland nodded.

"Patricia, James and Timothy are dead," said Flack.

"Murdered."

"We think Adam Yunkin did it."

"Murdered?" Sunderland repeated.

"And sexually mutilated," said Mac. "Patricia Mycrant was seeing you because she was a sexual predator."

"Yes," said Sunderland. "Court ordered."

"And the others?" asked Flack.

"Others?" Sunderland repeated, seemingly having trouble taking in what he was being told. "They were all sexual predators. My specialty. Adam isn't court ordered. He came in to see me on his own."

"Did they know each other?" asked Mac.

"Yes," Sunderland said. "We have . . . had a weekly group session here, in the next room."

"Anyone else in the group?" asked Flack.

"Yes, one more person. Ellen Janecek."

"I know that name," said Flack. "She's the teacher who seduced a thirteen-year-old student."

"Fourteen," said Sunderland. "He's sixteen now I think. She spent nine months in prison. Now she's out and fighting a relapse."

"Relapse?" asked Flack.

"She still wants to be with the boy. They're all dead?"

"Yes," said Mac.

"And Adam did it?" said Sunderland.

"Ellen Janecek," Mac reminded him.

"She's not making much progress," said Sunderland. "Normally I wouldn't be telling you all this about a patient, but—"

"Her address," said Flack.

Sunderland nodded and pulled a thick leather-bound notebook from his desk drawer.

"I've got everything on my computer but I keep

the computer in an alcove, right behind those doors."

He nodded toward the doors to his left.

"Patients don't talk as easily with electronics of any kind in the room. A computer is particularly intimidating. Here."

He handed Mac a sheet of paper on which he had written the addresses of Ellen Janecek and Adam Yunkin.

"What can you tell us about Adam?" asked Flack.

"Quiet. Hard to get him to talk. Close to impossible. Strange."

"Why?" asked Mac.

"He voluntarily joins the group and then says almost nothing. I'm going to . . . was going to give him another month or so and then tell him to either start participating or to see me on an individual basis. That he did not want to do."

"The limp," said Mac. "How did he get it?"

"War, he said, but he didn't say which war and I think there was something else. Something he didn't want to talk about."

"Thank you, Doctor," said Mac, rising.

Sunderland nodded in understanding. "I hope you find Adam before . . . This is horrible, isn't it?"

"It is," said Mac.

"You must see a lot of horrible things, people traumatized?" asked Sunderland.

Flack had now risen as well. He felt a twinge in his chest. Not quite pain. He resisted the urge to wince or touch the jagged surgical scar on his chest.

"I'm afraid so," said Mac.

Sunderland reached across his desk and took a handful of business cards from a shiny steel rack.

"I also specialize in dealing with people who have suffered extreme mental trauma. I treat many relatives of nine-eleven victims."

Flack looked at Mac, knowing that Mac's wife had been one of those victims, wondering if Sunderland had figured it out as well. When Sunderland held out the cards, Flack took them.

"If you come across any crime victims who could use my help . . ." the doctor said.

"We'll keep that in mind," said Mac.

Sunderland came around the desk. He accompanied the two detectives to the office door.

"This is horrible," he repeated, opening the door for them. "You think the media will—"

"Yes," said Flack.

"They'll find me," said Sunderland. He paused, considered this.

"Maybe that could lead to more referrals," said Flack.

"I wasn't thinking of that," Sunderland said defensively.

"Right," said Flack.

10

THE LIGHTS HAD BEEN turned off and the shades drawn in the classroom that had been the office/laboratory of Alvin Havel. Danny and Lindsay moved slowly, scanning the floor, tabletops, and desk with hand-held ALS devices.

"He took it with him," said Lindsay.

"Or put it back," said Danny.

"Back in the closet?"

"Back in the closet," said Danny.

"Good news is they're alive," said Devlin, standing at the edge of the pit. "Bad news is it looks like it's going to come sliding down on them sooner than we thought."

"How soon?" asked Stella.

"Don't know," said Devlin, taking off his helmet

and wiping his soot-darkened face with his sleeve. "Fifteen minutes. Maybe less."

"What are you going to do?" Stella asked.

"I'm going to go down there and get them out."

Stella wanted to say "no," but she couldn't. Hawkes was in that hole.

"The man who blew up this building is down there," she said. "He may have a gun. I'm a detective. I should go."

"Simple as that?"

"Simple as that."

"What would you do when you got there?" he asked.

"Whatever you told me to do to get them out," she said.

"No. You find killers and bombers. We go into burning buildings and flooded pits," said Devlin, waving at another fireman across the rubble.

"You win. Be careful," she said.

"I'm trained to be careful," he said. "Want to hear a crazy and totally inappropriate question?"

"Why not?" she said.

The fireman Devlin had waved to was on his way, carrying an armload of equipment and a rope coiled over his shoulder.

"When this is over, will you have dinner with me?"

Stella smiled. "Save my partner," she said. "Then we'll talk."

• • •

They had decided to split up.

Flack headed for the address Sunderland had given them for Ellen Janecek. Mac headed for the address for Adam Yunkin.

Adam Yunkin wasn't home. There was no home. The address he had given Sunderland was a phony, a gourmet food store on Lexington.

It got worse. When he got back to his office, Mac ran the name through more than a dozen databases. He came up with one Adam Yunkin, fifteen, Newark. Adam Yunkin was dead, a suicide. Hanged. Reason unknown.

A dead end except for one detail. Adam Yunkin had killed himself on June 16. Today was June 16.

Whoever was calling himself Adam Yunkin needed one more victim before midnight, one more sexual predator, into whose thigh he could carve that last *M* to spell "Adam."

Ellen Janecek was at home, a one-bedroom apartment in a subdivided Brooklyn brownstone. She opened the door when Flack knocked.

Flack remembered seeing Ellen Janecek on television during her trial and in the media interviews. Pretty, very pretty, long, straight blond hair, near perfect figure. On television she always appeared with a pleasant smile and a far distant look. That was the look that met Flack when she opened the door. She was wearing jeans and a tight black T-shirt. She was even prettier than she looked on television, but the look was not a seductive one.

"Miss Janecek," he said, showing his badge.

She held the door open and continued to smile blankly. He stepped in. She closed the door.

"I haven't been in touch with Jeffrey," she said.

"That's not why I'm here."

The room they were standing in looked like an ultraclean movie set. Bright flower-patterned sofa and two chairs, polished walnut dining room table with four chairs lined up. Flack was sure that if he measured the distance between them and their distance from the table, it would be exactly the same for each chair. There were color photographs on the wall, three of them, framed, about two feet by three feet. All three were of Ellen Janecek.

In one she was wearing almost exactly what she wore now. She smiled at the camera, thumbs tucked into her front jeans pockets. In another she wore a sleek, form-fitting red dress. Her hair tumbled across one eye. In the third, she sat in a chair, book open in her lap. She wore a prim skirt and white blouse and looked at the camera over her round, rimmed glasses.

"Nice photographs," he said. "Jeffrey like them?"

She didn't answer.

"Adam Yunkin," he said. "What can you tell me about him?"

"Why?" she asked.

"Because I'm going to ask you to pack some things and come with me so Adam Yunkin won't come here and find you."

"Why would he?"

"Because we think he may have killed the other three people in your therapy group, the one run by Paul Sunderland."

She shook her head, trying to clear it, trying to absorb what she had been told. "But . . ."

"It looks like he's going after people in the group. You're the only one left." He didn't add that by "one" he meant "sexual offender."

"No," she said.

"I'm afraid it's true," Flack said.

"No," she said. "I mean I'm not the last one. There's another one."

"Another one?"

"Yes," she said. "Another sexual offender. Paul Sunderland. He was arrested twice when he was twenty for allegedly molesting an eight-year-old boy. He wasn't charged or convicted."

"How do you know this?" asked Flack.

"He told us," she said.

"He's a psychologist. He couldn't—"

"He's a psychologist," she said, "but he's also a predator like the others. He doesn't have a license anymore. The others felt comfortable with a fellow offender, someone who knew how they felt. Joining the group was not mandatory. It was uncomfortable, but my lawyer said I should do it. I'm not a sexual predator, Detective."

"You're not?"

"No," she said. "I had a relationship with a fully developed young man. I didn't hurt Jeffrey and he was more than happy to be with me. As soon as he's old enough, we plan to be married and I'll work while he goes to school. Does that sound like a predator to you?"

"I don't make the laws," said Flack.

"Maybe you should," she said dreamily. "Maybe you should."

Flack flipped open his phone and speed-dialed Mac Taylor.

Outside a clap of thunder could be heard in the distance.

At least, thought Flack, the rain had stopped.

"Officer Maddie Woods, Brooklyn," Maddie said when she finally got put through to Danny Messer.

She had asked who was in charge of the Alvin Havel murder. The first person she talked to said she should call back tomorrow. The whole department was out dealing with looters, small disasters; assaults; the aftermath of an assault by nature.

Maddie hadn't given up. She pushed.

Finally she got Danny.

"Polish is all he talks," she said. "But we found a translator."

"And?" asked Danny.

"He says his son was diddling one of his students," Maddie said.

"He say which one?"

"Doesn't know," she said. "He says he tried to talk his son into stopping. Dark story. He says his son threatened the kid with a failing grade. She wasn't a virgin and Alvin was a good-looking man, but that was his father speaking. You know what I mean. Was he?"

"Good looking?" said Danny, imagining the dead man with his face in a pool of blood on his desk and red pencils sticking out of his neck and eye. "Not the last time I saw him. Does Havel's wife know her husband was having an affair with a student?"

"Waclaw, the dad, doesn't know," said Maddie. "Want me to talk to her, see what she knows?"

"Yeah, thanks."

"She know her husband's dead?"

"Yes."

"I'll take Waclaw home and talk to the widow."

"Thanks, Woods."

"Nothing," she said. "It gives me an excuse to get out of this office and see the damage. I'll call you if I find anything."

"Anything," said Danny.

"Right down to the victim's shoe size," she said.

A row of thick, empty glass containers that looked like test tubes with flat bottoms were lined up in the storeroom at the back of the chemistry lab. The containers were empty, waiting for an experiment that might never take place.

Danny and Lindsay began by lifting every container from the shelf and inpsecting it with their ALS units. Less than ten minutes later Lindsay held up something that looked like a clear, thick-walled peanut butter jar with a heavy base.

"This could be it," she said.

Danny moved over to look. Turning the light on the jar they saw the telltale dark dots that signaled blood. Small. The killer probably thought he'd wiped off all the blood. He was wrong.

Holding the jar at the bottom, Lindsay unscrewed the top and inserted her fingers inside. She turned the jar upside down and they both examined it. The bottom was rough, chipped, with traces of blood.

"Used the jar like a hammer," she said.

"Some glass had to get on whoever drove that pencil in his eye," Danny said.

"Maybe even blood," Lindsay said.

"Get that back to the lab," Danny said. "See

what you can find. I'll bring the representatives of the future of our country back for tea, cookies and more conversation."

"Anything else we should be looking for? If there is I'd like to find it before I have to make another trip."

Danny stepped out of the storeroom and stood next to Lindsay, who had placed the jar in a evidence bag and marked the time, date and location on the label.

"We spend half our time just driving from scene to scene and to the lab," Danny said. "That's a fact. There was a study. Mileage was checked. Travel time was checked. Half our time."

"That's a fact?" she said.

"That's a fact," Danny said, deadpan. "Would I lie to you, Montana?"

"Never," she said.

"That's why our evidence kits keep getting bigger and bigger," he said. "So we can run more tests in the field and don't have to do as much moving evidence to the lab."

"And I thought it was about new forensic technology," she said.

"We live and learn, Montana."

"I'm enlightened," she said. "Thanks."

"You're welcome," he said. "Give me a call if you find something."

• • •

"It's been bad for Keith," the woman said into the phone.

"He and Adam were close," Mac heard a man say on an extension.

Both Eve and Duncan Yunkin sounded as if they were at least seventy. Mac knew that they were both fifty-three, but it had been a hard fifty-three years.

"If Keith were here when Adam—" she began.

"He couldn't have been," said Duncan. "He was out of his mind for more than a month. The leg."

"The leg," Eve Yunkin said. "Shattered."

"They cut it off," said Duncan.

"How did it happen?" asked Mac.

"He was working in Africa," she said. "Security work for Klentine Oil. They're British."

"He was a mercenary, plain and simple," said Duncan.

"His Jeep turned over," Eve said.

"He ran into a wall," Duncan said impatiently.

"Spent four months—"

"Five, almost six," he said.

"In rehabilitation. When he got out, there was some trouble."

"Trouble? He beat up three men in a bar," said Duncan. "Almost killed two of them. He said they were homosexuals who tried to pick him up. He went to prison for it. One year."

"Do you know where your son is?" asked Mac.

"Adam is dead and buried," said Duncan Yunkin. "Dead and buried. He killed himself."

Mac could hear the man's wife sobbing.

"I meant Keith," said Mac.

"Who knows? We haven't heard from him in more than nine months."

"Eleven months and one week," his wife said.

"Did he and Adam stay in touch?"

"Adam wrote," Eve said. "They would tell each other things they'd never tell us."

"Last question," said Mac. "The three men he attacked in the bar. What did he use on them?"

"His fists," said Duncan.

"And the little knife," she added.

"And the knife," Duncan concurred.

"What kind of knife?" asked Mac.

"Army Ranger knife," said Duncan. "Stainless steel, fit in the palm of his hand, opened with a flip with either hand. Keith was always fascinated by knives. I don't know why. He showed it to us. Is he dead too?"

"I don't think so," said Mac.

"Then what's the problem?"

Your son has murdered three people, Mac thought. And I think he's about to try to kill a fourth.

"Why did Adam kill himself?" Mac asked.

"Depression," said the boy's father.

"Depressed about what?"

"We don't know. The doctors didn't know. They said it was teenager stuff. Loneliness. Loss of a sense of self-worth. Humiliation by a girl. Lack of friends. There's a name for it. I don't care what the name of it is. Giving it a name won't bring Adam back. That answer your questions?"

"Yes, thanks," said Mac.

"He hurt some more people, didn't he?" Duncan asked.

"It looks that way."

"If you find him . . ." Eve trailed off.

"I'll have him get in touch with you," said Mac.

He could hear the woman crying softly. Someone hung up the phone.

You can't protect a person if you can't find him. By the same token, whoever was trying to kill Paul Sunderland probably couldn't find him either. Mac was reasonably sure that the someone was Keith Yunkin.

Twenty minutes later, in Sunderland's apartment, which was in the same building as his office, Mac watched the therapist throw some things together into a worn leather garment bag, including cuff links and two watches, one of them a Movado, a real one, not a knockoff you could buy for fifteen bucks from a midtown sidewalk stand.

"I could just take a train or get a flight out of town," said Sunderland. "I could stay in touch and you could tell me when you've caught Adam."

"His name is Keith," said Mac. "Adam was his brother."

"I don't understand," said Sunderland.

"He wasn't a sexual predator," said Mac. "He was pretending to be one."

"I see," said Sunderland, "but why can't I—?"

"We don't know what his resources are," said Mac. "I'd say he's very resourceful. We'd like you where you can be under police protection."

"And if I don't want to be?" asked Sunderland.

"We'll insist," said Mac.

Mac used Sunderland's computer and found a Web site that sold military knives—American, German, British, Italian, you name it. Mac named it and searched the photographs. Two fit the rough description Keith Yunkin's father had given. Mac called the number on the site. It was for an address in Queens. He ordered six knives at twelve dollars each and told the woman who took his order that he needed them sent to the crime scene lab by courier.

"I'm not sure . . ." the woman who took his order said. She sounded young. She sounded New York.

"I am," said Mac flatly. "I'm a police office investigating a murder and I want to stop another one."

"I'm sending it," the woman said. "Cash, check or credit card?"

He gave her a credit card number and expiration date.

Mac glanced out of the window. Even though the rain had stopped, the sky was still dark, rumbling, ominous. The black clouds moved quickly in from the ocean, threatening to release again. Water was still ankle deep or higher in the streets.

Was it a June afternoon? Was it really nine years ago? He had taken an afternoon off. They had gone to the Central Park Zoo to watch the penguins. His wife was a penguin person. He was a seal person. They had been in no hurry. People passed them as they sat eating peanuts, saying nothing, deciding without saying it that this was a special day and they should celebrate with her favorite, Thai food. And then it had rained. Suddenly. They had been caught. Soaked. No umbrella. No cabs would stop on Fifth Avenue. Traffic was bumper-to-bumper and filled with frustration. They went to the apartment, stripped, made love. Eight years maybe. A June afternoon.

An hour after he had called to place his order, Mac sat in white lab coat and carefully sheared off slivers of stainless steel from the tip of an Army

Ranger knife. It was painstaking, slow, absorbing in its detail.

He almost forgot about that day in June.

Jackson Street was flooded, knee-deep, like many other streets in Queens. Kids in shorts had stripped the wheels from old skateboards and were trying with little success to surf down the empty streets.

The water was overflow, sewer backup, filthy and dangerous. There were warnings on television and radio, but the kids of Queens were not paying attention. They were having fun.

Sam Delvechio screamed, "Get out of my way," and, board in hand, ran through the dark water as fast as he could. Then he plopped stomach down on the board and sailed surprisingly quickly down the middle of the street. He was going in the direction the water was flowing.

His friends Doug and Al took their turns, gulping in bacteria and laughing.

"Look," Al called out.

A fish, about a foot long and moving against the flow, swam down the street.

"Catch it," Al called.

They grabbed for the fish, but couldn't hold it.

"Hit it with the board," called Sam.

Doug swung at the fish with his board, missed. Al took a turn and hit the fish, which was just getting the idea that it wasn't safe. It sped up.

Sam took a turn, hit the fish. The fish turned on its side, still swimming. Sam was about to strike again when he stepped on something. No surprise. He was barefoot in the middle of the street.

He was about to swing again when Al said, "Hey look."

Blood curled up to the surface of the dark water in front of Sam.

Sam reached down and groped for whatever it was he had stepped on. The fish righted itself and swam away. Sam came up with something that looked like, and was, one of his toes.

"Hey, shit," said Al.

Sam looked dazed and said, "It doesn't hurt."

"Get your aunt," said Al. "They can sew it back on."

"My aunt?" asked Sam, staring at the bloody toe in his hand.

"No, Sam," said Al, whose father was a paramedic. "The hospital."

Doug stepped forward, reached down into the murky water, cautiously moved his hand along the surface of the street and touched something. He lifted it and held it up.

The open blade of the Army Ranger knife was stained with blood.

It had been dark during and before the rain, but it was even darker now. Somewhere behind the ominous clouds and rumbling sky the sun was going down. Night was coming.

"My first name's John," said Devlin as the board was eased into the pit by two other firemen.

The board was blue, plastic, two and a half feet wide and seven feet long.

"Stella," she said.

"Stella," he repeated. "I'll be right back up with your partner."

"Be careful," she said.

There was a metal coil hooked to the fireman's waist. Devlin had removed his raincoat and put on a long-sleeved plastic jacket.

Stella nodded and Devlin straddled the board. The two firemen at the surface started to ease him down by slowly releasing the coil as Devlin slid into a darkness broken only by the light mounted on his hat.

The sides of the pit bled dirt and debris around him.

Standing near the edge, Stella watched the light bob into the blackness and grow smaller as the fireman descended.

Stella turned her eyes to the taut metal line and the two men who were easing it down. The line went slack and Devlin's voice called, "I'm down."

There was little room for movement at the bottom of the pit. Hawkes was kneeling and holding Custus's head out of the water. In the light from his lamp, Devlin could see the injured man's pale face. The man wasn't dead. Not yet.

"Doctor?"

"I'm okay," said Hawkes.

There was "okay" and "okay." Devlin had seen them all. He looked at the beam that trapped Custus's broken ankle. He unhooked the metal coil from his waist and reached over to hand it to Hawkes. Hawkes shook his head.

"You'll need my help," he said, nodding toward Custus.

"I know how to do this," said Devlin.

"And I know what his body can take. Let's get it done."

It was Devlin's turn to nod.

"What're you nattering about?" said Custus, eyes closed. "Can't you see a man is trying to reach nirvana here?"

"He has a morbid sense of humor," said Hawkes.

"I'm not easily amused," said Devlin. "Let's get him out of here."

He reached into the water, found the rubble under Custus's ankle.

"Can't move the beam," he said, pulling his hand out of the water. "We have to try to clear enough room under that ankle to pull him out."

"Let's do it," said Hawkes.

"Let's do it carefully," said Devlin. "The beam

is wedged tight. It's not going to shift, at least not because we remove some of what's under it. Slow so more debris doesn't slide down when we work."

"There's an irony here," Custus said weakly, painfully, as the two men reached under his broken ankles. "But it eludes me."

"Under the circumstances," said Devlin, "that comes as no surprise."

"Ahhh." Custus groaned in pain as a chunk of plaster the size of a football crashed into the water near his head. "This," said Custus, "is the moment in which I am to nobly tell you to save yourselves and leave me to my fate, but I have a secret."

"More than one," said Hawkes.

"Well, yes, but you've penetrated some of my better ones," Custus said. "No, the secret is that I'm not afraid to die, but I am very curious about the future I'll miss if I do. Ah, the irony. Now I remember. You are risking your lives to save me so that I can be accused of a bevy of crimes including murder. If brought to trial and convicted, I will spend what remains of my life in what . . . ?"

Neither Hawkes nor Devlin answered.

"In a dark pit," Custus supplied.

"Might be clear," said Devlin, leaning back, knowing that they had been lucky so far, knowing there was only so much luck to go around for a fireman. "Let's try it. I'll take him under the arms and pull him slowly. You ease his leg under the beam. Let's do it."

"Wait," said Custus. "Doctor, you wouldn't have something a bit stronger than those pills to knock me into oblivion?"

"I've already given you enough morphine to knock out a horse," said Hawkes.

"Did you? Well, it must have been a Shetland pony. I suppose there's no recourse other than to pass out or suffer. The choice now belongs to whatever gods may be who hold dominion over my impenetrable soul."

"Now," said Devlin.

They moved him. His ankle didn't quite clear the beam. Hawkes moved Custus's legs to the side, both hands on the ankle to feel where the bone was most vulnerable to further fracture.

A wave of water seeped in from the jagged wall where the dark open part of the cellar had been minutes earlier. Devlin's beam fell on Hawkes's face. Hawkes shook his head. Both men knew that they were working against a ticking clock that had only a few minutes left.

"Do your best," said Devlin. "We're trying again. And this time it works even if it isn't pretty."

Devlin renewed his grip under Custus's arms as Hawkes reached into the water under the beam.

"Okay," said Hawkes.

"Now," said Devlin, pulling.

"Sweet Secret Jesus," screamed Custus.

Hawkes turned the ankle as Devlin pulled.

Something cracked in Custus's leg.

"Let me be," he said. "You torturous—"

"You're clear," said Hawkes.

Custus didn't hear. He'd passed out.

"Quickly but carefully," said Devlin tying the coil around Custus.

The two men eased his dead weight in the awkwardly tight space. They moved slowly, fighting the urge to hurry, an urge that could get them all killed.

"Ease him up," Devlin called to the two firemen above. "He's not conscious."

The coil went tight and the limp, dripping man was hauled on the board slowly upward until he was no longer visible.

"You're next," said Devlin.

Hawkes didn't argue. When the coil came down, he helped Devlin put it around his waist. Then Hawkes reached for his kit. He had placed Custus's gun inside the kit next to the other evidence he had gathered. Custus had not been all that wrong in the assessment of his situation. The difference was that Sheldon Hawkes did not see the irony.

"Let's go together," said Hawkes.

"Too heavy," said Devlin. "I'll see you on solid ground."

Hawkes felt the pull around his chest as the coil dug in and he was lifted upward into twilight and the waiting face of Stella, who reached over with one of the firemen to help him over the brink.

"You need a long shower," she said with a grin as he stood on more-or-less solid ground.

Across the bombed-out remains of Doohan's, Hawkes saw an ambulance that had to be carrying Custus pull away down Catherine. The ambulance lights were spinning. Half a block farther the siren began to blare.

Stella and Hawkes both watched the coil go back down the hole, clacking against the plastic board. A sound like the belch of a giant echoed from below.

The coil dropped farther, went taut, and the two firemen pulled. Slowly, Devlin appeared. He was helped over the edge by the two firemen who had pulled him up.

Devlin looked over at Stella and grinned.

Stella grinned back.

The monster from below bellowed and went silent.

The walls of the pit did not suddenly collapse. Days later the hole remained and was finally covered over by a bulldozer, which flattened what was left of Doohan's Bar and left the space free for a well-equipped workout center. It would be called Doohan's Gym.

• • •

The hotel Ellen Janecek and Paul Sunderland were taken to for the night was barely a two-star accommodation. Sunderland offered to pay for an upgrade to another hotel, but Mac had no time to make the move and besides, there were no other rooms available. People had been trapped by the deluge. Rooms had been gobbled. In other cities, the people might be irritable, complaining. In New York, they were resigned. New Yorkers were no strangers to disaster.

Sunderland and Janecek had been transported to the hotel by Don Flack, who had made sure that they were not followed.

Neither of them had objected, not when Mac gave them a hint of what Keith Yunkin had done to the three other people in the therapy group.

Both of them had been told to stay in their rooms, use room service, make no phone calls. A uniformed officer was in place outside each of their doors.

"How long will I have to do this?" Sunderland had asked.

"Till we catch him," said Flack.

"What? A day? Two days?"

"I don't know. Enjoy the HBO."

Ellen Janecek hadn't asked how long. She had nodded affirmatively to everything Flack said. She smiled that I-have-a-secret smile that made him uneasy, then announced she was going to take a shower.

Flack named her Beautiful Dreamer. Mac thought it fit. Flack had left her after she locked the door behind him.

He nodded at the burly dark cop outside her door. She was safe. At least for tonight.

When she got out of the shower, Ellen's cell phone was ringing. She had been told not to make calls. She hadn't been told not to answer them. Besides, it was an automatic response on her part. The phone rings, you answer it.

"Hello," she said.

"Ellen, I gotta see you. Where are you?"

The line was bad, very bad. She could barely make out the words.

"Jeffrey?"

"My mom's . . . tonight . . . never."

"I can't hear you," she said.

"Please," he said. "Where are . . . got to . . ."

"The Hopman Hotel," she said. "You know where it is? Can you get here?"

"Room?"

"Four seventeen," she said.

The line went dead.

He was in trouble. Jeffrey was in trouble. Jeffrey needed her. She couldn't turn him away. She wouldn't turn him away. She loved him.

It was a little after nine. Mac rubbed his eyes, touched his face. He needed a shave. The lights flickered in the lab and made a crackling sound before returning to full strength.

The storm was over, at least for now, but the standing water in streets, gutters and basements was shorting out electrical circuits. Subways stalled. Dirty rain gurgled up from sewers, and the rats, sniffing at the now-clear air, were rushing more boldly along the sides of buildings in search of food.

Stella had called, told him the firemen had gotten Hawkes out safely. The force of Mac's relief had been strong and it made everything a little easier to deal with on this wet and dismal day.

Mac leaned over the table again and reached for a dropper. He put the dropper into a solution he had prepared with the shavings from the knife tip that had been taken from the body of Timothy Byrold.

He walked across the room and placed the specimen into a spectrograph. Less than a minute later he had the information he needed. He couldn't tell the age of the stainless steel, not with certainty, nor could he be sure of the exact corrosion rate because of the dozen factors that affected corrosion. What he could tell was the level of corrosion and the composition of the samples of stainless steel Sid Hammerbeck had taken from the wounds of the victims. If he found the knife the minute flecks of metal had come from, it would be easy to match them. The composition of the stainless steel and the level of corrosion would match the sample to the knife like a fingerprint. In addition, the microscopic ridges of the knife would match the ridges made by the knife when it struck the bone of each victim.

And Mac was about to seek that match now.

The knife that cut off the toe of the boy in Queens lay on the lab table. The hospital had turned the knife over to the police. The knife was an Army Ranger knife, not all that unusual. But what was unusual was that it was scalpel sharp, which accounted for its going cleanly through the boy's toe. The Queens detective who had taken the knife remembered the bulletin, marked urgent, about three sexually mutilated victims who had been murdered with sharp, stainless steel. The detective had dropped the knife in an evidence bag and sent it to the CSI lab in Manhattan.

Now it lay next to Mac Taylor, who had found enough blood on the blade to make a type match to Byrold. There was even more blood from another source. Mac assumed it was the injured boy. He called the hospital in Queens to check on his type, was told it was a match, and that the boy's toe had been successfully reattached.

"Kid says he wants the knife," the nurse Mac talked to said. "Says he found it and it's his."

"Tell him it's evidence in a murder case," said Mac.

Mac was definitely tired, but there was no going home. Nothing waited for him there but troubled sleep. Out there a man named Keith Yunkin who walked with a limp and had murdered three people was seeking a fourth victim before midnight, before the anniversary of his brother's death was over.

Mac checked the preliminary autopsy reports on the three murder-mutilations. The data on the cleanest wounds, the initial ones under the victims' armpits, did not match. He checked again. The difference was small, but it was there. Mac was sure they were accurate. Sid wouldn't make a mistake like this, not even a small one.

He picked up the phone and called the medical examiner's cell phone.

"Sid?"

"Mac."

"Where are you?"

"With friends," said Sid. "Colleagues who have a few beers and stronger fare and share tales of the dead."

He wasn't drunk, but he had managed to take the edge off.

"The three you did today—"

"Excluding the teacher with the punctuation marks in his neck and eye?"

"The other three," said Mac.

Someone called Sid's name. Sid covered the phone and Mac could hear him say, "I'll be right there."

"Could all three have been killed by different weapons?" asked Mac.

"Interesting question," said Sid. "There was a slight difference in the shearing from the wounds under the arms. I attributed that to—"

"He could have sharpened the knife after each murder," Mac supplied.

"Right," said Sid. "Or the tissue of each victim could have accounted for a difference in shearing, but . . . now that you mention it. I think I'll go back and take another look at the departed."

"It can wait till tomorrow," said Mac.

"I can't," said Sid.

He hung up and Mac sat back.

A clean, new, scalpel-sharpened knife for each victim. Ritual execution? No ripping. Methodical. Not simple revenge. He's ridding the world of sexual predators. And there's no reason to think he'll stop at four or stop at the end of today.

11

THE MAN SAT AT THE BACK of the subway car, his lips moving, making no sound. He wore a poncho and hood. The hood was drawn forward. His face wasn't visible. His hands were plunged into his pockets.

There weren't many people on the train, not at this hour, not heading back into the city, not on a system that had been damaged by stalling and flooding.

What few people were on the train sat away from the hooded man who held one leg out awkwardly, bouncing nervously. They were New Yorkers. They were familiar with the crazies who talked to themselves and to people and creatures who were not there. As long as they didn't talk to you, you could live with it.

The hooded man's voice could now be heard but

only when the train came to a stop at a station. What he said made no sense, though the word "kill" was heard by some.

Two people got off at the next stop even though it wasn't theirs. They would wait for the next train, though it might take an hour, and hope that those aboard it were reasonably sane and safe.

On the train, the man in the hood grew more restless and angry at whatever ghost or demon with which he argued.

Edward Bender, tired before he even began his night shift at the Colston Hotel, was getting increasingly aggravated by the mumbling man, but he wasn't sure what he could do about it.

Suddenly the hooded man rose with a roar and started down the aisle, moving awkwardly. A heavy white woman cried out something in a language Edward didn't understand.

The hooded man had a knife in his hand. It didn't have a long blade, but the blade did glisten in the flickering subway light. The train swayed and the hooded man started up the aisle. Edward rose, threw his magazine on the seat. The hooded man was as tall as Edward and younger, but Edward no longer gave a shit.

Passengers were cringing against the windows, covering their faces with their arms or closed umbrellas.

"Are you washed in the blood of the lamb?"

the hooded man asked Edward. The man was no more than a few yards from Edward, who said nothing. The man's right arm rose, clutching the knife. He lunged forward at Edward and fell to the floor. Edward stomped on his hand. The knife slid down the aisle.

"Oh, thank God," someone said.

Edward looked at the man seated on the aisle. The man's leg was still in the aisle. He had tripped the hooded man and possibly saved the life of Edward Bender.

"Thanks," said Edward, a foot on the neck of the hooded man who screamed, "We've all had enough. The deluge. No time for an ark."

"I'll stop the train at the next station," Edward said. "You find a cop."

Keith Yunkin, who had tripped the hooded man, nodded, got up and moved to the door just as the train pulled into the station. He stepped out onto the platform.

It would take him a little longer to get to Ellen Janecek, but he had a few hours. It would be enough.

He moved toward the exit. He had no intention of finding a policeman and he hoped that no policeman would find him.

Lindsay should have been home taking a hot bath and eating one of the ripe peaches she had set aside for herself. Instead, she sat before a monitor in the CSI lab looking at this morning's surveillance tapes of the Wallen School. A cup of chili and a Diet Coke rested next to the monitor.

She looked at everything, paying particular interest to the images of the corridor outside the chemistry lab. This was the fourth time she had scanned the tape looking for—she didn't know what she was looking for. It was a feeling. She had feelings like this from time to time. Sometimes she was right about them. The Loverton poisoning the first week she came to New York was one example. Most of the time the feeling didn't pan out, either because she couldn't find the forensic evidence or she was simply mislead by her instincts. This effort with the tapes looked as if it wasn't going to pan out.

Then the glitch. She saw it and knew even before she proved it to herself. Lindsay saved the screen and opened a word processing program. She typed in the sequence of the camera shots, the order in which the camera picked up the images. There were sixteen surveillance cameras randomly programed but carefully positioned in the Wallen School. Lindsay typed in data on all sixteen. She didn't have to check to be sure she was right, but she did check.

She went back to the morning tapes, pausing to wolf down spoonfuls of chili and wash them down with Diet Coke. No doubt about it. The corridor outside the chem lab was not in the tenth sequence. She went through the next sequences looking for the corridor in each one.

The corridor was missing in the eighteenth sequence.

It hadn't been a mystical feeling. She had seen and sensed that something was not right in the tapes. Now she had proved it.

Each sequence had a time in white letters on the first image. The tenth sequence read: 8:40 a.m. The eighteenth sequence read: 10:50 a.m.

The missing video of the corridor was from ten minutes before Alvin Havel's last class to a few minutes after the class ended.

She had questions to ask now. Who had access to the monitor security room? Who had the expertise to erase and manipulate the tape? What had been deleted and why?

Lindsay finished the chili, threw the empty carton in the nearby trash, took her Diet Coke and headed home where she planned to reward herself. She would dare to eat a peach.

Driving to Queens was a nightmare. Taking the subway would probably have been worse. Flack had listened to the police band reports. Just a few minutes earlier a train had been stopped on the way in from Queens when one of the passengers tried to attack the others with a knife. The passengers had subdued him, but the line was delayed for almost thirty minutes while police made their way to the scene.

Flack shook his head. This trip might lead to nothing, but what else did they have? He had an address for Dexter, the Umbrella Man. He had a full name, Dexter Hughes. Dexter lived in Queens with his sister, Larissa, an LPN and a gospel singer with a bit of a local reputation.

This had been told to him by Alvino Lopez, who owned the garage on 101st Street where Dexter got his umbrellas. Alvino did not know Dexter's address, but that had been no problem for Flack. The problem had been that no one had answered the phone at the unlisted number of Larissa Hughes, which meant a trip to Queens.

Roads were leading to Queens. Dexter. The boy who lost his toe. The knife that took it that Mac said was the murder weapon. No, alter that. It looked now, according to Mac, as if it was one of the murder weapons. Keith Yunkin seemed to have an arsenal of sharp and deadly knives.

Flack arrived at the small frame house a few minutes after ten. Just about that time Keith Yunkin was getting off the subway at the Thirty-fourth Street stop, four blocks from the hotel where Ellen Janecek was patiently checking her makeup for the fifth time in the past hour.

• • •

"You all right?" asked Stella.

"I'm all right," said Hawkes. "A few bruises. What have we got?"

"Dead people," she said.

They were in the crime scene lab, papers neatly overlapping and laid out, an image on the monitor, a simplified room with four thick, black supports in each corner. Three shapes were placed inside the room. Two together in the middle, another at the far right. Two others were placed outside the room on the left.

"That's the cook on the right," said Stella, moving the arrow to the figure.

Stella maneuvered the arrow on the screen with the mouse and said, "The beams in each corner of the room went together. TNT."

An animated spark flashed. Hawkes nodded.

"Beams buckled, ceiling collapsed," she said.

With that the ceiling of the room on the screen fell and covered the shapes in the room.

She clicked again and the already bent and twisted support beams buckled and collapsed. The three figures were gone.

"FDNY arson investigator says the placement of the bombs was perfect, professional," Stella said. "But the kind of material used, the amount, suggested an amateur."

"Someone wanted it to look like the work of an

amateur, but they also wanted to be sure Doohan's and everyone in it went down," said Hawkes. "Why? Custus looks like a professional. Some of those scars on his chest and arms are twenty-five years old at least. Question is still there. Why pretend to be an amateur?"

"I don't know," said Stella. "I'm running DNA on everyone who died in Doohan's and on Custus. Maybe we've got a bomber besides Custus."

"Two in one building at the same time," said Hawkes. "Quite a coincidence."

"Don't believe in them," Stella said.

She turned back to the computer screen and began typing.

"Okay, all three people in the bar look up."

The stick figures on the screen moved their heads.

"Then Doohan and Custus come in."

Two stick figures enter the image from the left. The first figure falls. The ground opens and swallows the second figure.

"Powder, explosive burns and residue on Custus," said Hawkes. "He shot Doohan, fell into that pit."

"Doohan has powder burns on his hand too," she said.

"Whose gun is it?" asked Hawkes.

"Street gun. Registered to a pawn shop owner in Dearborn, Michigan," said Stella. "Reported stolen five years ago."

"Street gun," said Hawkes.

"How do you see it?" Stella asked.

"More questions. If Custus planted those bombs, and it's pretty clear he did, what was he doing standing around outside the bar just before he detonated? He could have been killed."

"And," added Stella, "what was he talking to Doohan about and why did Doohan run into the bombed-out bar? Did Custus shoot him? Did Doohan shoot himself? Why?"

They sat looking at the screen. Then Hawkes flipped through the lab reports.

"We can ask Custus," he said.

"He'll tell you?"

"He thinks he's smart," said Hawkes.

"Is he?"

"Yes, but maybe he can be fooled. We've got something on our side he doesn't have."

"What's that?" asked Stella.

"Science."

The woman was tall, round, and black with smooth skin and glasses at the end of her nose. She could have been any age between forty and seventy. Flack thought that "handsome" would be a good word to describe her.

She stood blocking the door, arms folded. He showed his identification. She did what few people did. She checked the photograph, looked at him and then back at the photo before nodding her head to show that she was satisfied.

"Larissa Hughes?"

She nodded again.

"You know why I'm here, don't you?" he said.

"Pretty sure," she said, "but I'd like you to tell me so I don't step in a hole I didn't have to dig."

"Your brother, Dexter," said Flack. "Can I come in?"

She stepped out of the way.

"Prying eyes," she said. "Good-looking white man comes calling at night on a weekday and people will talk. Fewer who see you the better."

He stepped in. She closed the door behind him.

"Dexter's in the living room pretending he's watching girls playing softball."

Flack followed her through a door on the right and found himself looking at a thin black man, seated on a sofa, his head cocked to one side, a gun in his hand.

"It's not him," Larissa said.

"I know, but maybe he sent him," said Dexter, aiming the gun at Flack. "Don't move fast and don't reach under that jacket. I've been through two wars, lost one eye and plan to live to sell a lot of umbrellas."

"He's the police," said Larissa.

"Sure?"

"Certain," she said. "Put the gun away."

He slowly placed the gun on a table next to the sofa.

"You saw the man who killed Patricia Mycrant."

"Who?"

"Woman murdered on the roof above the Brilliance Deli."

"Shit," said Dexter, turning away and shaking his head.

"Tell the man, Dexter," his sister said.

"Man's crazy. I talk, he finds out who I am. He comes over here and slices me unless I get lucky and blow him all to shit. I'm not feeling lucky."

"You know who he is?" asked Flack.

"I know," Dexter said with a sigh. "I don't know his name, but I know."

"How do you know him?" asked Flack.

Dexter hesitated.

"He's killed three people," said Flack. "We've got a lot of reasons to believe he plans to kill another one tonight."

"Seen him coming out of the building with all the apartments," said Dexter. "The yellow one with the dirty bricks, the one your friend said the face of Jesus was on in the dirt. No one believed her."

"Dorothy is harmless," said Larissa. "Tell the man what he needs to know."

"I just told him. I seen the man coming out of there maybe ten, fifteen times, maybe more."

"Where is the building?"

"Three blocks down," said Larissa.

"Take him out and put him away," said Dexter. "If he sees me again, one of us is going to die and the odds are good it won't be him. I'm sixty, shaky and one-eyed. He's young and limpy and I won't be easy to catch, but he'll just keep coming. He's . . . What do you call it when you see in someone's eyes that he won't give up till you put a silver bullet through his heart?"

"Relentless," said Larissa.

"Right," said Dexter. "Relentless."

Lindsay and Danny sat in a narrow pizza shop that promised Chicago-style pizza. In Chicago they promised New York–style pizza. In Boston they promised Philadelphia-style pizza.

"Can't be sure it was a girl," said Lindsay.

They were sharing a small sausage pizza.

"No," said Danny seriously. "After all, his friend Wayne O'Shea caught him coming out of the closet."

"Funny," she said, grabbing the last pizza slice.

"Want another one?" he asked.

"You?"

"Let's live dangerously."

"My treat," she said, getting up.

"Only fair," he said. "You eat twice as much as I do."

When she got back, he reached for a slice before she could place the pan on the table. He grinned and adjusted his glasses. They were the only customers. The place smelled of grease and grilled meat. Danny felt at home.

"Have you talked to Hawkes?" Lindsay asked.

"Just for a minute. He sounds fine. Tired."

"He's not the only one. We should both get some sleep," Lindsay said.

"I forgot," said Danny. "Back in Montana you get up before the cows."

Lindsay began working on a pizza slice and said, "We get a lot done while you're still sleeping. You want to go back and go over the files again?"

Danny shrugged.

"One of those kids knows who was in that closet," he said. "So . . ."

"We look for boyfriends, girlfriends, angry parents, brothers, sisters," she said. "Long list."

"We look for anyone who has residue glass in their palms," he said.

"Let's go back and make a list," she said.

"Bring the rest of the pizza with," Danny said.

"A party."

"Not exactly," he said.

Lindsay had a vivid moment of recall, the dead teacher with the pencils protruding from his neck and eye. Then, another image, an older one from before she had come to New York, an image that came unbidden.

"Not exactly," she agreed.

• • •

The courtyard building was clean, well lit. The
panel of names and buttons looked new, metallic. Most of the name plates next to the buttons
were filled in, neatly printed. None of the name
plates read "Yunkin" or anything like it. There
was, however, one plate that read: THIBIDAULT,
MANAGER.

Flack pressed the button next to the name. No
response. He pressed again. Then he put his thumb
on the button and didn't let up until he heard a
voice, tinny and distant, say, "Come back in the
morning."

"Police," said Flack.

"Crap," sighed the tinny voice. "Coming."

A few seconds and Flack heard something on
the other side of the solid wood door. There was
a slightly larger than standard peephole. The eye
that appeared was wide open.

"Hold it up," said the man beyond the door.

Flack held up his ID, knowing there was no way
the man could possibly read it through the hole.
The door opened. The black man who stood there
wore dark slacks, a green shirt and a matching
green cowboy hat. He also held a pair of sunglasses
in his hand.

"Poker night," the man explained. "Just heading
out."

He was no more than five foot five and weighed no more than a hundred and fifteen pounds.

"I'm looking for a man. Late twenties. White. About my height. Walks with a limp."

"Melvoy," the little cowboy said.

"Melvoy what?"

"No," said the man. "Lee Melvoy. Apartment Two-A right over mine. What's he done?"

"Is he in?"

"Heard him go out about an hour ago, maybe less. What's he done?"

"I'd like to take a look in his apartment," said Flack.

"Don't you need a warrant?"

"I've got one."

"What's he done?"

Flack showed him the warrant. He had picked it up from Judge Abbott a few hours earlier. It gave no address, but it read, "the residence of one Keith Yunkin."

"He's a quiet guy."

"Jeffrey Dahmer was a quiet guy," said Flack.

"Yeah. Melvoy do something bad?"

"Looks that way."

"Knives," said the cowboy.

"Knives?"

"He sells 'em. Shop on Stoneman. All kind of knives. Says right on the window, 'Bohanan's Collectables, Combat, Cutlery.' Works there. Guns too. He stab somebody?"

"Let's go look at his apartment so you can get to your poker game, cowboy."

When they got to the apartment, Thibidault opened the door, reached in and hit a switch. A light came on in the overhead fixture in the middle of the ceiling.

They stepped inside.

The one-bedroom apartment was as clean and sparse as a monk's cell. Flack had seen apartments like this. He had even seen a monk's cell. Monks get murdered too. Not often. Sometimes monks are murderers. Not often either.

"Keeps it clean," said Thibidault. "I wish all the tenants were like him."

"Be careful what you wish for," said Flack.

The living area held one straight-backed wooden chair with curlicue arms. The chair faced a low dresser atop of which was a fifteen-inch television set. Next to the chair was a wooden-topped desk table with black metal folding legs. In a corner to the left was a cot covered by a sheet under a khaki blanket. The blanket was pulled tight. A pillow rested at the head of the cot. The pillow showed no sign of wrinkle.

There was one thing on the wall and one thing only. To the right of the cot was a framed black-and-white photograph of a teenage boy and a crew-cut young man. The boy's hair was tumbled over his forehead. The man had his arm over the shoulder of the boy. The photograph had been blown up as much as it could bear without losing the image to grain.

"That's him," Thibidault. "The older one, only he don't smile, never saw him smile. I don't know who the kid is. Okay if I go now?"

"The kid's name is Adam," said Flack, moving toward a closed door to his left. "And no, I'd appreciate it if you stayed."

Thibadualt sighed deeply.

Flack might want a witness, depending on what he found or didn't find. The impatient man at his side wouldn't be much of a witness, but he would be better than none at all.

Flack moved to the closed door, opened it and reached over to turn on the light.

"Never been in there," said Thibidault. "Not since Melvoy moved it."

A small plywood desk sat in the middle of the room. On top of the desk was a computer that hummed in sleep mode. Against the wall to the right were floor-to-ceiling bookshelves. Simple. Planks nailed neatly together. Magazines, neatly lined up, were piled on the lower shelves.

On the wall to the left were two old, battered, unmatched display cases with glass windows. Behind the glass windows were neatly displayed knives, none large, most in sheaths or folded closed. There were about two dozen of them. Through the glass panes Flack could see that the blades that were visible were sharp and glistening.

On the back wall was corkboard on which a series of photographs had been pinned with small plastic push pins.

"Who're they?" asked Thibidault.

Flack looked at the photographs of Patricia Mycrant, James Feldt, Timothy Byrold, Ellen Janecek, Paul Sunderland and another woman and four more men. At the bottom left-hand corner of the photographs of this day's victims was a red check mark.

"Some friends of your Mr. Melvoy," said Flack, moving to the bookshelves, Thibidault at his side.

Flack picked up a magazine. Thibidault looked over his shoulder as he flicked through the pages of *Beautiful Children* magazine.

"Jesus Christ, he's a perv," said Thibidault.

"No, he was doing research."

"Research?"

There was a wireless phone on the desk next to the computer. Flack picked up the phone and pressed the redial button.

"Jeffrey?"

"No, Ellen, it's not Jeffrey," said Flack. "It's Detective Flack."

"My mistake," she said.

"A big one," said Flack. "Did you get a call from Adam Yunkin?"

"No," she said.

"From Jeffrey?"

She didn't answer.

"Did you tell him where you are?"

No answer.

"Get out of that room," said Flack. "Now. There's a policeman outside your door. Get him."

"But . . ."

"Get him," Flack demanded.

"Wait," she said. "There's someone at the door."

"Don't . . ." he shouted, but she couldn't hear him. She had put the phone down.

12

CONNOR CUSTUS WOKE UP looking at the ceiling of a
dimly lit hospital room. He was feeling no pain but
he knew that his lack of agony was only a result
of the temporary solace of medication. He didn't
know what they had given him, but it was working. His own drug of choice under comparable
circumstances in both the recent and past had been
morphine.

Connor welcomed the haze, knew that all he
had to do was close his eyes and he would be
asleep again, but such was not to be. He caught a
movement to his right and turned his head to see
a vision, a beautiful woman who reminded him of
a girl in a Sicilian village whose name escaped him
at the moment. The girl in the village was a beauty.
So was the drug-induced vision at his bedside.

He began to close his eyes again when a voice said, "Custus."

He recognized the voice, the policewoman who had been at the rim of the pit, Hawkes's partner.

"A mistake has been made," he croaked, throat dry, slightly sore from dampness and the dust of a dead building.

A straw touched his lips. He drank. The water moistened his throat and tongue.

"A mistake?" Stella asked.

"I'm in heaven being served by an angel," he said. "That is certainly a mistake. I belong elsewhere. I'm not complaining, mind you, but if the system fails at this level, than how far behind is total chaos in the universe? I assure you my question is philosophical and not rhetorical."

"You like to talk," said Stella, standing above him.

"It's cultural and genetic," he said. "Most of the people in the inbred town I came from in Australia like to talk, take pride in it, get little work done because they're so enamored of their voices and words."

"Good," she said. "We have a lot to talk about."

"I'd prefer to wait till dawn," he said. "I can promise a greater coherence and willingness then."

"I'd prefer you less coherent and less willing at the moment," she said.

"Let me guess. Irish and Italian," Connor tried.

"I'm Italian and Greek," she said. "And you are not Australian, you're Irish and in trouble."

"Ah, when was I not? How is the good doctor?"

"Doctor Hawkes is fine," she said.

"Send him my regards."

"I'll let you do that yourself tomorrow. Want to tell me what happened?"

"By 'what happened' I assume you mean the murky events of this morning before I was swallowed by the sullen earth."

"That's right."

"Memory fails me," he said, flexing his fingers, starting to feel life in them. "Trauma does that sometimes. I fear I'll never remember. Selective amnesia."

"Then I'll tell you," she said, sitting in an uncomfortable blue naugahide chair.

Custus tried to turn his head toward her, but she was now just out of sight. He could hear her voice as he had in the rain-filled hole, in the darkness just hours ago. Was it hours? How long had he been here? Damn. He was waking up. There would be pain now unless he got more medication, agonizing pain in his broken ankle, numbing pain in his side.

"I'll listen better with something to quell the coming pain in my broken limb and wounded body."

"When I finish," Stella said.

"You're tired," said Custus.

"I'm tired," she agreed. "Want to hear my story?"

"Bedtime story?"

"Something like that."

"Then by all means, though the promise of a powerful narcotic would make me a much more attentive listener," he said. "And I gather that's what you want."

"It's what I want," she said. "I'll call the nurse when I'm done."

"Then by all means launch into your tale."

"You were hired by Doohan to blow up the bar," she said. "He told you the bar would be empty in the morning, that it usually was except for the cook and that the days of rain would keep even determined morning drinkers away. Worse case, Doohan said he'd get rid of the customers, tell the cook to go home because of the weather."

She looked at Custus, who said, "Not quite, but close enough if it were reality and not a tale."

"You planted the explosives the night before. Why didn't you bring the bar down then?"

"If I were telling this fanciful tale," Custus said, "I would say that Mr. Doohan had no alibi for the night, but he had a perfectly good one for the morning when he was supposed to be sitting in the barbaric chair of his dentist, whom he had called with an emergency. The telling touch would be that the dentist would confirm that Doohan did, indeed, have an emergency, a missing filling, an open nerve."

"But . . . ?" said Stella.

"Ah, let's see," said Custus. "What if the dentist were not in, what if the storm of the century canceled his office hours?"

"What if?"

"He might go to the bar as he did every day," said Custus. "He might, if the tale were true, wait for me to come, try to stop me, get me to put off the sweet experience for another day."

"But he didn't," said Stella.

"Let's, to keep the conversation going and not deprive me of the company of a beautiful woman, let's assume he did not? Water?"

Stella reached over, took the water-filled paper cup from the bedside table and held it out to Custus who pursed his dry lips over the straw.

"Refreshing," he said. "So, we return to the tale?"

"So, alibi gone, Doohan hurried back to the bar knowing you were going to bring the place down. You argued in the street. He had a gun, the one Doctor Hawkes found you with. It's registered to Doohan. I'd guess he kept it behind the bar. The two of you argued. You went into the bar. He shot you. You took the gun from him and shot him. A shot hit the wet dynamite. Wet dynamite has been known to go off at the slightest spark, sometimes even spontaneously."

"A bit too fanciful here for me," said Custus. "I believe I'm falling asleep."

"I'll keep you awake," Stella said. "The story gets better, much better."

"How could it?"

"You had talked Doohan into hiring you to blow up the bar," she said. "You probably gave him a very good price for your services. My guess is you tricked him into providing a paper trail, probably increasing his insurance."

"Why would I do that?"

"Because you weren't doing it for the money he was paying you."

"I didn't do it at all," he said. "I just like talking, imagining that—"

"Detonators?" she said. "You purchased detonator caps through a low-level drug dealer named DJ Riggs. He can identify you."

"A drug dealer," Custus mused. "They make fine witnesses, I'm told."

"This one's a hero. Saved a baby's life this morning."

"You have the imagination of Rabelais. Down a dark and winding road into a forest wherein dwells an avatar, an avenging angel by the name of Stella. Now, if you would, I'd like that medication and a long sleep. And in the morning, I should like to

open my eyes and see not your beauty but the face
of an attorney assigned to defend me. In any case,
much as I love talking, I'm going to close my eyes
and dream of you."

"Connor Custus," she said, "you are under arrest for the murder of . . ."

And even without the comfort of medication,
he closed his eyes and was asleep.

Ellen Janecek went to the door of the hotel room.

She checked the dead bolt and resisted the urge
to look through the small glass circle in the door.
She had seen a movie in which a man had put
his eye to one of those peepholes. A single shot
had come through the hole and burrowed into
his brain. She had also seen a television episode
in which a man had gone to a door after someone
knocked and was torn to pieces by a shotgun vol-
ley through the thick wood panels.

Ellen stood at the side of the door and said,
"Who is it?"

"Message from the front desk," came a male
voice.

"What is it?"

"I don't know. An envelope dropped at the desk.
Man asked that it be delivered to you."

"What man?"

"I wasn't on the desk when it came."

"Slip it under the door," she said.

"I don't think it will fit."

She looked down at the bottom of the door. There was about a quarter of an inch opening.

"Try," she said. "If it doesn't fit, just leave it in front of the door."

"I can't do that," he said.

"Then take it back to the desk."

Something scuttled by the door and a thin, white envelope poked under the small opening.

"Anything else I can do?" he asked.

Maybe he was just waiting for a tip. He wasn't going to get one, not if it meant opening the door.

"Nothing," she said.

"Right," said the man.

She pressed against the wall and listened. The thin carpeting masked his footsteps. She thought she heard a slight jingle, maybe keys in his pocket. The sound moved away. She reached down, pulled the envelope in and quickly pressed herself back against the wall next to the door.

She did not panic. Panic was not part of her being. Caution was. He had almost tricked her. She should have known that the call had not come from Jeffrey. She should have known it wasn't his voice no matter how much the caller had tried to hide the truth. But she loved Jeffrey. There was no question about that. She was no child molester, not like the others in the group. This was unfair, but she had grown used to life being unfair.

She tore open the envelope.

The note inside read: "Ellen, Another time. Another place. Adam."

"Mr. Sunderland. Police."

Paul Sunderland had been reading a book, Thomas Friedman, *The World Is Flat*. Well, he had been trying to read it, but he kept imagining the mutilated bodies of the three people who had been in his group only two days ago. He kept imagining the man he had known as Adam, the quiet, calm man who listened thoughtfully as other people talked. He could imagine Adam standing over Patricia Mycrant with a knife in his hand. What he could not imagine was what the police had said Adam had done with the knife.

Paul got up, put the book aside. The hotel room smelled musty. He hadn't brought his inhaler. It would be a long night, a sleepless night.

"Yes?" he called.

"We think Adam Yunkin is in the hotel," said the policeman. "He just left a note for Miss Janecek."

"How did he—?" Sunderland began.

"He called her cell phone. She told him where she was. We've got to move you both to another location. Detective Flack is on the way."

"Oh shit," mumbled Sunderland.

"Let's go," the policeman said urgently. "Leave your things. We'll have someone bring them."

Sunderland was still dressed but barefoot. He moved to the door and said, "I've got to get my shoes and then . . ."

He opened the door.

Somehow he wasn't surprised. Did he know, suspect at some level that he would be facing Adam Yunkin? Paul was at least as big as the man he knew as Adam. Paul was also in good shape. Forty minutes each morning at the gym, twenty of those all out on the stationary bike. The man he had known as Adam didn't appear to be armed, but Paul knew that was certainly not the case.

"Come in," Paul said calmly.

Keith limped into the room, closing the door behind him. Could Paul lure him farther in, away from the door? If he could just get him away from the door, Paul could beat him into the corridor. Where the hell was the real cop, the cop who was supposed to be guarding him?

"Let's talk," said Sunderland.

"About what?"

"You," said Sunderland.

"Nothing to say," said Keith.

They stood facing each other. Keith stood between Paul and the door.

"I didn't molest that boy," said Sunderland.

"You're lying," said Keith evenly.

Sunderland shook his head and said, "No. The boy lied. That lie changed my life, almost ruined it."

"In the sessions, you said—" Keith began.

"I needed the confidence of everyone in the group if I was going to help them. I needed your confidence. I never got it."

Keith Yunkin hesitated.

"You're lying to save your life," he said.

"No, I'm telling the truth."

Sunderland's eyes met Keith's. He was convincing. Paul Sunderland made his living by being convincing. Keith was not convinced. He took the knife out of his pocket and flipped it open.

Sunderland played it out, eyes meeting Keith's with sympathy he really felt and with fear, which he hid.

Paul made his dash for the door. Paul didn't make it.

Mac got to the hotel lobby just before Flack arrived. When they got off the elevator on the sixth floor, they found Mike Danielson, the uniformed officer who had been guarding Paul Sunderland, kicking against the door of a linen closet in which he sat, hands tied behind his back. His head was a hood of blood.

"Didn't see him," Danielson muttered as Mac

pressed a gauze pad from his kit against the wound.
"Did he . . . ?"

Flack untied Danielson quickly. Then he joined
Mac, who was headed for Sunderland's room. The
door was closed but not locked.

Paul Sunderland lay on the musty carpeting,
pants and underwear pulled down, shoeless, head
turned to his left, looking at nothing.

"What do you see?" asked Flack.

"Rage," said Mac, wiping blood away from the
dead man's thigh. "And this."

Flack looked over the kneeling Mac's shoulder,
saw the letter *M* cut deeply into the flesh, checked
his watch and said, "He got it done in one day, the
anniversary of his brother's death, *A-D-A-M.*"

"One question left," said Mac.

"What?" asked Flack.

"Is he done spelling?" asked Mac.

13

MORNING. THE MAN KNOWN AS JIM PARK, whose name had been Jung Park before he legally changed it, was late for work. He had never been late, not in the six years he had worked for Sunstar Digital Service Laboratories. Damned subway. He would explain the situation to Walter Parasher, whose name before he legally changed it was Akram, which meant "most generous," which Jim sincerely hoped would be his guiding principle when Jim walked tardily into the office.

It would have helped if Jim were not considered to be the company comic. It would have helped if Jim's efforts at jokes were appreciated or understood by his Indian bosses, particularly Walter. It did help that Jim was brilliant, though he often feared that his skill was not enough to save him in

a downsizing. What he did came easily to Jim and
so he doubted his value and assumed others could
easily do what he did. They could not.

Jim was an electrical engineer, a research engineer whose task was to use computer technology
to chart patterns in the billions of stars around us,
and to locate new stars and galaxies.

Jim never looked through a telescope. Remote
scanning devices around the world fed data into
the company's computer network and Jim, in his
office in Manhattan, separated the noise and dirt
of the universe from the objects of interest.

Jim was thirty-nine, recently married to an Irish
American woman named Sioban, who was already
pregnant.

Twenty minutes ago, he had stood on the
platform in the damp for forty minutes, people
jostling, coughing, bumping into him. Jim was a
patient man, but he had to get to work.

In his hurry, when he got off the train at Union
Square, Jim had stepped onto a piece of cardboard
in the gutter. His foot had gone through the soaked
cardboard and into six inches of filthy water that
now clung to his socks and squished inside his
shoe.

Inside the office building now, he recognized
no one going for the elevator. None of the familiar
faces. They must all have made it on time. How
had they done it?

The elevator doors closed. Only two others in the car. They knew each other, and seemed to be in no hurry. One was a pretty woman in her forties in a black dress and a very broad belt. The other, a man in his fifties, stocky, well dressed, his shoes and feet not wet and reeking of filth. Did they smell the mess on his pants, socks, inside his shoe?

Jim was breathing hard. He had used his inhaler fifteen minutes after he got to the subway platform. It was a little too soon to use it again, but it was an emergency. He did not want to face Walter reeking and wheezing.

He reached into his pocket for the inhaler and his cell phone to check for messages and found something else, something hard, metallic, something that had not been there an hour ago.

Jim pulled the object out and held it before him, adjusting his glasses. There were brown spots on the otherwise gleaming metal. He looked at the other two people on the elevator to see if they were watching. Jim knew what he held. What he did not know and did not expect was that he had just touched something that flipped open the razor-sharp, blood-covered blade of the knife.

The pretty woman saw the knife in his hand. She let out a sound, not quite a scream, more like an inflated balloon whose mouthpiece had been pulled tight. The man noticed now. He had a briefcase. He reached into it, fumbled for something.

"No," said Jim, knife in hand.

The man took his hand out of the briefcase. He was holding a very small gun. The woman was behind the man.

"I don't—" Jim said.

The man with the briefcase shot him.

It wasn't a fatal wound or even a very bad one. The small bullet entered his left shoulder and stayed there.

Jim dropped the knife and slumped back against the elevator wall as the doors opened.

"Don't move," said the man, his voice quavering. And then to the woman. "Get help."

It was just a little after ten-fifteen and already the worst day of Jim's life.

For some reason, the meaning of his Korean name, Jung, came to mind. Righteous. His name meant righteous. He felt not the least bit righteous at the moment.

The silver and black metal box about the size of a small carry-on sat on the desk, its cover swung open. Lindsay plugged the black fiber-optic cable into the box. At the end of the cable was a switch and a 400-watt lamp. She set the dial in the box to one of the six wavelength settings. The wavelength she selected would reveal even minute fragments of glass when the light was on. Then she selected a pair of orange goggles.

They were seated in a conference room connecting to both the corridor and the headmaster's office at the Wallen School. Walnut table and twelve matching chairs. Portraits of Wallen's four previous headmasters and one previous headmistress on the walls.

Danny wasn't impressed, which would have been a minor disappointment to the board of Wallen, which had spent almost ninety thousand dollars to make the room look impressive and a little intimidating.

"And that will do what?" asked the headmaster, looking at the metal box on the table.

Headmaster Marvin Brightman looked as if he had beaten out at least ten contenders for the role of headmaster in a movie about prep schools. He was perfect, lean, tailored suit and tie with blue and white stripes, a cloud of white hair, an intense, handsome dark face.

"It'll help us in our investigation," said Danny.

"Can you be a little more specific?" Brightman asked. "They are going to ask."

"We'll give them an answer," said Danny.

"It wasn't easy to get permission from the parents," Brightman said.

"But you got it," said Danny, sitting.

"I told them, as you suggested, that it is in the

best interest of Wallen, the students and the parents, to resolve this situation as soon as possible and eliminate their students of all suspicion."

"And they'll all be here?" asked Lindsay.

"They'll all be here," said Brightman.

"They believed you," said Danny.

"They thought that I was giving them a line of total bullshit," said Brightman. "These are not stupid people. But they didn't have much choice other than to refuse to cooperate, which would make their children look guilty."

"So they aren't happy with you right now?" asked Danny.

Brightman shook his head and smiled.

"Detective, you have a gift for understatement. The only people they are less happy with than me is the two of you. The difference is that you can live with their displeasure. I have to deal with it. My ass may well be on the line. Will you be done by eleven?"

"Yes," said Lindsay.

"Good, we have an assembly scheduled at that time to honor Alvin Havel's memory. It would be good if you had his killer in hand by then, not that I have any great expectations of that. I have a school full of frightened people."

"No guarantees," said Danny.

"I didn't think so."

"Let's get started," said Lindsay.

"Let's," said Brightman.

Danny and Lindsay had arrived at nine and met with Bill Hexton, the Wallen security officer in the empty school lunchroom over coffee.

"Who has access to the video room?" Danny had asked.

"Me, Joe Feragmi and Liz Henning, both half-time security," Hexton had said, shaking his head. "Joe's retired NYPD. Liz was a deputy in the sheriff's department in Westchester. She got married last year. Husband's an architect."

"And that's it?" asked Lindsay.

"No," said Hexton. "Joe and Liz can get in there with their pass key, but so can Mr. Brightman and whoever's on the night cleaning crew."

"Who else?" asked Danny.

"Everyone," said Hexton, adjusting his tie. "We don't lock the door during the day, just close it. A student, a teacher, a secretary could go in."

"So that narrows it down to everyone," said Danny.

"Yes," said Hexton. "Sorry. We've never had any reason to—"

"How long would they have?" asked Lindsay. "In the video room before someone saw them?"

"Not long," said Hexton. "Ten minutes max. Not enough time to doctor the tape and you couldn't be sure one of my people didn't show up, but . . ."

"But?" said Danny, reaching for the coffee carafe.

The coffee was good, but what would you expect at the Wallen School?

"Yesterday was crazy," said Hexton. "I was on alone when Mr. Havel was killed. I don't think I was in the video room for more than half an hour all day."

"And the door was open?" asked Lindsay.

"Unlocked," said Hexton. "We've never had a problem with the video room before."

"You've got one now," said Danny.

"Big time," Hexton agreed.

"Any of the students in Havel's class know enough tech to alter the tapes?" asked Lindsay.

"All of them, probably," said Hexton. "It's not that hard. It just takes a little time."

"How much time?" asked Danny. "How long would it take someone to make those changes to the tape?"

"I don't know. . . . Maybe twenty minutes. Maybe fifteen."

"Anyone fooling with the tapes ran the risk of being caught in the act, right?" said Danny.

"Not if there were two of them," said Lindsay. "One to alter the tape, the other to watch for security to return."

• • •

The call from Mac came while Stella sat in a chair at Connor Custus's bedside. She had more questions for Custus, who pretended to be asleep.

Custus had seen a soft orange-red when Stella focused a light on his closed eyes. There was no rapid eye movement under the lids, no vibration to show that he was dreaming. What she did see was a slight occasional movement that told her that Custus was faking.

She could have called him on his deception. She could have turned him over to the district attorney's office, but she had questions and she knew she was unlikely to get anything from the man other than more games and lots of talk. Stella was patient, but she was also tired and the chair was not comfortable.

When her cell phone rang, Stella quickly checked the charge in her battery. It had enough. She checked the caller ID and said, "Mac."

"How's it going?"

"A few loose ends," she said.

"Tie it up. I need you on the mutilation case."

He quickly brought her up-to-date. She listened, glancing at Custus who had turned his head almost imperceptibly so that he could better hear the conversation.

Stella asked questions. Mac answered patiently. Custus listened.

"I'll be right in," she said.

"No," said Mac. "Just go to the elevator. Take it up to six and go to room six-oh-three."

"What's there?" she asked.

"I am. We've got a possible lead. He was shot."

"The killer shot him?"

"It's more complicated than that. Come up and I'll explain.

"Hawkes?"

"He's back at the lab with a knife our wounded witness found in his pocket."

"His pocket? The killer put the knife in his pocket?"

"He did," said Mac. "And I'm hoping that it was a big mistake."

"I'll be right up."

She clicked off her phone and Custus, eyes still closed, said, "I gather from your end of the conversation that you have one very sick whelp you're trying to bring to ground."

"Yes," said Stella.

It happens sometimes. More often than Stella wished it. She would track down a murderer only to find that she felt sorry for him or her or even liked the person. Connor Custus, if that was really his name, was responsible for the death of four people and who knows how many before that. True, he had not meant to kill anyone in Doohan's, but the law called it murder. Still, Custus was a charmer.

"I'm somewhat of an expert on murder for

revenge," Custus said. "I've worked for and with organizations that exist for the sole purpose of vengeance. It's all relative. They tend to be dull and mirthless fanatics and no fun at a pub or poker table."

"Your point?" asked Stella.

"Murder weapon in the pocket of an unwary and randomly selected traveler. I've actually seen just that before. It's all relative. Why this traveler's pocket? Because he had a wide and open pocket? And why not just throw the weapon away? Why take a chance on being caught in the act of reverse pocket picking?"

"Why?" asked Stella.

"Because," said Custus, "he wants to be caught. He has a message to deliver to the world about the wounds he has suffered and he will continue to send that message through his murders until you catch him and give him a martyr's forum. He leaves messages, doesn't he?"

"Are you a psychologist, too?" she asked.

"Oh, far better and worse than that," he said with a smile, looking directly at her now. "But it's all relative."

Hawkes had spent three hours in bed after showering, shaving and making himself a protein shake. He couldn't down solid food, not yet. He hadn't slept. Each time he started to fall asleep he had felt the sudden sensation of falling, rapidly falling backward into darkness, knowing that if he didn't wake up he would keep falling until he was too deep to awaken.

He had sat up moist with sweat, hyperventilating.

The phone had rung and Mac asked him if he were up to going to the lab and examining the knife he had recovered from James Park. Hawkes welcomed the excuse for getting up and out.

He had showered again.

He knew the symptoms. He knew what was wrong. He would continue to feel the urge to clean himself, try to get rid of the imagined and real darkness of the damp pit he had shared with Custus. He could prescribe something for himself, probably would but he knew he would also have to deal with that fear he did not want to face, the fear of being entombed in an avalanche of filthy water and sharp-edged heavy slabs of plastic, plaster, metal and dead rats.

If he was not better in three days, he would seek help, short-term patch-up therapy. The department had good people, good therapists. The problem, he knew, was that he would know what they would say and what they would try. It was the curse of being a physician. In the long run, even with help, it would be a matter of physician heal thyself.

The best thing to do was to lose himself in work and Mac had just offered him the opportunity.

Hawkes finished dressing. He had a knife to examine.

Waclaw handed the diary to his widowed daughter-in-law. The children, Thad and Clara, were playing video games in Thad's room. They had been told that their father had died. They had been told that it was an accident. The trick would be to keep the truth from them, an impossible trick given the ready availability of the Internet, emails, television news, friends who found out, newspapers. They were young, but they would, when they were older, find out. She would have to talk to them about it but Anne didn't know how or when.

Her father-in-law was no help. He sat in front of her, his heavy lids drooped, his eyes moist. She understood no Polish and Alvin was no longer alive to translate for her.

The diary was on her lap, a clothbound book with the word "Journal" in black letters on the cover. Men called it a journal. Women called it a diary.

The word "Journal" was the only thing written in English. The rest of the journal was in Polish in Alvin's no-nonsense, highly legible but incomprehensible block letters.

"You know I can't read this," she said.

She was tired. She longed for the rain to return and set up a protective dark waterfall around the house. If someone had covered her eyes and said, "Quick, which dress are you wearing?" she wouldn't have been able to answer with more than a vague guess.

"He says her," Waclaw said.

"He says her?"

"Uh-huh."

He held up both hands, fingers splayed. Then he made a fist and opened his fingers again. Then he pointed at the journal.

"Page twenty?" she asked.

He didn't know the word twenty so he reached over and flipped pages. Alvin Havel had numbered the pages in the upper right-hand corner. Waclaw tapped the open page with a lean finger.

"Hers," he said.

Waclaw knew he looked like a fool. In Poland, he was considered to be a fine speaker, a union spokesman, a man his son, when he was alive, had been proud of. Waclaw knew he should have made a greater effort to learn English, but Alvin spoke perfect Polish. Waclaw's grandchildren spoke no Polish.

"Dzieweczyna," he said pointing to the page.

"Dizwezna?" Anne repeated.

Close enough, thought Waclaw. Dzieweczyna. He didn't know the English word "girlfriend," but her name was in Alvin's journal. Well, not her name exactly, but the name he had given her in Polish. He pointed to the name.

Nogi.

"Her name is Nogi?" asked Anne.

"Niech pomysle."

Waclaw pointed to his legs, then ran a hand down each of them.

"Legs?" Anne asked. "Nogi? Legs?"

Waclaw shook his head "yes" and sat back exhausted by his effort. "Legs."

Annette Heights was the first student through the door of the conference room. A tall man with hair as dark as hers stood behind her. She was still cute. He wasn't. He wore a blue suit, carried a briefcase and had a face that did not promise a smile.

It wasn't Robert Heights, the concert pianist, who Danny would have been happy to meet. This man was all lawyer and no more than thirty years old.

"John Rothwell," he said, pulling out a chair for the girl who smiled up at him.

Danny wondered if she thought Rothwell was cute too.

No one shook hands. Rothwell and Annette Heights sat at the table. She looked at the metal box with the black cable and the orange goggles.

Rothwell didn't look. He had a very good idea of what they were.

"What are you looking for?" Rothwell asked.

"Glass," said Danny.

"Glass?"

"Glass," Danny repeated.

"Why?"

The girl seemed to be amused. Her lawyer wasn't.

"Evidence that would go a long way toward removing your client from any possible suspicion," said Danny.

"Clients. I represent all of the students on behalf of Wallen School. And if we say 'no'?"

"We ask a judge to step in," said Danny. "Won't look good. Could get out to the press."

"Cut it out, John," Annette said with a sigh. "Let them do it and let's get out of here. Where are you looking for the glass? You want me to undress?"

"Not necessary," said Lindsay. "Just your hands."

"All right," said Rothwell. "But they'll answer no questions."

And they didn't, nor did Lindsay and Danny ask them any.

It went faster with the other students in Alvin Havel's chemistry class, James Tuvekian, Karen Reynolds, Cynthia Parrish. No trace of glass on any of their palms.

"Let's check the boyfriends," said Lindsay after

the students and their lawyer had left. "Someone was in that closet. Someone watched for security to come back when the tapes were being altered. Someone's got glass in their palm."

Jim Park sat propped up in bed. A pretty woman with an Irish face and red hair, his wife, stood on one side of the bed. Stella and Mac stood on the other side. Park's wife touched her husband's shoulder. He winced.

"I'm sorry," she said. "I forgot."

"I wasn't going to hurt anyone," Park said. "I didn't even know the knife was in my pocket."

"We believe you," said Mac.

"They believe you," Park's wife said reassuringly.

"Good, then they can be witnesses," Park said. "I'm suing the man who shot me. Sioban, get me a lawyer."

"What kind of lawyer?" she asked.

"A mean one," he said.

"Mr. Park," Mac said. "We've got a few more questions."

"I did not have a good morning," Park explained.

"We know," said Mac.

"Ask your questions."

"Any idea when the knife was put in your pocket?" asked Mac.

"Yes, between nine-thirty and ten-seventeen.

I was late for work. I reached into my pocket to check my cell phone messages at nine-thirty. I was on the train platform. The next time I checked was ten-seventeen in the elevator. That's when I found the knife in my pocket."

"See anyone suspicious near you?" asked Mac. "Anyone bump into you?"

"Everyone was suspicious-looking, even me, and everyone bumped into me. No one says 'I'm sorry' or 'Pardon me.' Wait, one man on the platform who bumped into me did say 'Sorry.'"

"What did he look like?" asked Mac.

"What did he look like?" Park's wife prompted.

Park looked at her with mild exasperation.

"I don't know," he said. "Just bumped into me, said 'sorry' and limped into the crowd."

"Which train stop was it?" Mac asked, looking at Stella who rubbed the bridge of her nose and closed her eyes for a few seconds.

"Gun Hill Road, the Bronx," Park said.

"Gun Hill Road, Bronx," his wife repeated.

"Where's your jacket?" asked Mac.

"Over there," said Park, gesturing at the closet a few feet away.

"I'll need it," said Mac.

"Keep it," said Park. "It's got a hole in it where that guy shot me."

"Blood too," said Park's wife.

Mac nodded.

Gary House was, more or less, Annette Heights's boyfriend. He was, like her, a junior. According to Annette, Gary was her best friend.

"He's smart," she said. "He's quiet, except when he gets excited about computers, and he likes to be bossed around."

"And you like bossing?" asked Lindsay.

"Love it," she said.

Gary House was pudgy, pink cheeked and straw haired. He was quite willing to put his hand out to be checked.

"There's a newer model," he said, looking at the metal box. "Detects a dozen substances."

"Too expensive," said Danny.

"Technology is always ahead of forensic economics," said Gary House.

"Okay," said Lindsay.

He pulled his hand back and placed it in his lap.

"You have chemistry with Mr. Havel?" asked Danny.

"Everyone has chemistry with Mr. Havel. There's only one chemistry teacher in the Wallen School. He had the market cornered."

"That all he had cornered?" asked Danny.

"Gary," John Rothwell warned.

Gary House looked at Danny blankly and then at Lindsay, who said, "He corner any of the girls? Annette, for example?"

"No," he said emphatically. "She would have liked it if he tried though. She likes to flirt."

"I noticed," said Danny.

"Gary," the lawyer said. "No more talking."

"Can I go now?" the boy asked.

Lindsay nodded. Gary had no trace of glass in either palm.

Karen Reynolds's boyfriend, Terry Rucker, was not a nerd. He wasn't a fool either. It took a little persuasion by Headmaster Brightman to get him into the conference room.

"Hands," said Lindsay.

Terry reluctantly put out both hands. He was several inches over six feet tall and well built. His shirt was about half a size too small to show off his upper torso.

"Palms up," Lindsay said.

He complied.

Lindsay turned the light on his hands.

"Is this dangerous?" Terry said.

"No," said Danny. "Where were you at ten yesterday morning?"

"When Mr. Havel was killed, right?"

"Right."

"Terry, you don't have to answer any questions," Rothwell said with a hint of resignation.

"In Ithaca, at a basketball game."

Lindsay could see no sign of glass, but there was the residue of something on his palms.

Cynthia Parrish did not have a boyfriend. She did, however, have a close friend, a very close friend, on the cross-country team. Jean Withrow was black, model lean and pretty. Her hair was pulled back and tied tightly. She wore a blouse and a skirt that revealed lean, powerful legs.

"I'm not telling you anything," she said, sitting and folding her arms across her chest.

"We haven't asked you anything," said Danny. "But I am now. Please hold out your hands."

The girl looked from Danny to Lindsay, then at Rothwell, who nodded to show that it was all right. She shook her head and held out her hands.

"You hurt me, my father sues," she said.

"Painless," said Lindsay.

"I know why you had me brought in here," Jean said. "You think Cyn and I are suspects because we're gay and Havel hit on me."

"Jean," Rothwell warned.

For someone who wasn't going to talk, Danny thought, she was providing a whole lot of information.

"And what did you do when he hit on you?" Danny asked.

"Looked at him cold."

She showed them the look. It was very icy indeed.

"Then I told him if he laid a hand on me again, I was going to scream 'rape.' And I also told him that if I got anything lower than the A I deserved, he'd be looking for another line of work."

"And what'd he do?"

"Ceased and desisted."

"Didn't threaten to 'out' you?" asked Lindsay.

The girl smiled. Nice smile. "Everybody knows we're gay. Even my family and Cyn's. They are, to use their words, 'cool with it.'"

"Are they?" asked Lindsay.

"No, but there's not much they can do and they live in hope that it will pass like the flu."

"Yesterday, ten to eleven in the morning?" asked Danny. "Where were you?"

"Spanish class. No lo creeo?"

"We'll check," said Danny.

When the girl had gone, James Tuvekian's two closest friends were examined. Neither showed signs of glass fragments in the palm.

The last three people called in were Bill Hexton and the other two security guards.

Epidermal samples were taken from everyone. No glass fragments anywhere.

"Looks like we'll have to do the whole school, Montana," said Danny, sitting back, hands behind his head.

"Maybe not," Lindsay answered, starting to pack the machine away.

There was something. Lindsay wasn't prepared to mention it, not till she got back to the lab. The palm of one of the hands they had looked at was puffy, slightly sore and had a slightly green residue. The other palm looked normal. She had taken a swab from the suspicious palm.

14

"WHAT HAVE WE GOT?"

The question was put by Mac Taylor, who leaned back against his desk. Stella and Hawkes sat in front of him. Flack leaned against the wall. They were all beyond tired.

"We've got someone watching his apartment," said Flack.

"He won't go back," said Mac.

"No," Flack agreed. He put his hand to his face. He needed a shave. He needed a shower, hot water beating against his aching back. He needed some sleep.

"Evidence?" asked Mac.

"The knife in Park's pocket is the same one used to kill Paul Sunderland," said Hawkes.

"Man has a lot of knives," said Flack.

"He made a mistake," said Hawkes. "There were traces of something interesting on the handle and in Park's pocket. Paint. Green. Fresh."

"How fresh?" asked Mac.

"Fragments are still pliable," said Hawkes. "He wasn't painting walls but he did lean against one that wasn't completely dry. Paint is a blend. High end. Expensive. Mixture of three colors. It comes out mostly green. I talked to the manufacturer. It's not used in homes much. Marketed to high-end office buildings, doctors' offices, law firms, places like that."

Hawkes had taken the paint chips to the paint store, which had computer color-matching software. They had taken the paint chip, placed it in front of a small detection window on the computer that then identified the proper formula to make that particular color. It took no more than a few seconds. The formula was displayed on the computer monitor. With the push of the "enter" button, the clerk at the computer could have created a gallon of paint that exactly matched the small chip Hawkes had supplied.

"The paint was purchased by Norah Opidian & Associates, Office Decorators," said Hawkes. "I called their number. Answering machine says they're closed, at a big office decorators' convention in Philadelphia."

"Keep trying," said Mac. "Call the convention

hotel. See if you can find somebody who can help you find where that paint came from."

Mac pushed away from the desk, turned his head and looked out the window. The room went silent for a moment.

"Everything's connected," Mac said finally. "We have to find out how. He put the knife in Park's pocket at the Gun Hill station. What was he doing there? He doesn't live there and neither did any of the people he killed."

"He's not done killing," Stella said, rubbing her eyes.

"He's not done killing," Mac agreed.

Pulling her thoughts from Custus was more than difficult and Stella knew why now. It had come to her a few minutes ago when Mac was looking out the window. Custus reminded her of Tom O'Brien, the administrator at the orphanage when Stella was ten years old. O'Brien and Custus had the same Irish accent, the same wit, though Stella had not been able to really understand it when she was ten. One day Tom O'Brien had simply been gone and no one would say where. The rumor was that he had been caught touching one of the girls.

He had never touched Stella. Or had he? The image of a smiling Connor Custus came to her. Custus was reaching out to touch her.

"Stella?" said Mac. "You with us?"

"Yes, sorry. Yunkin may not be finished spelling," she said.

"The day is over," said Hawkes. "He wanted to get his brother's name carved into four child molesters."

"We're lucky his brother's name wasn't Anthony," said Flack.

No one laughed.

"But his brother had a last name," said Stella. "And there was one other person in Paul Sunderland's therapy group."

"Ellen Janecek," said Flack.

"And his brother's first name could be repeated," said Stella. "There are a lot of child molesters out there."

"The anniversary of his brother's death is over for this year," said Hawkes.

"He could be planning to spend another special day carving out a name for himself," said Flack. "His brother's birthday maybe."

"Birthday? When was Adam Yunkin's birthday?" asked Mac.

Flack took out his notebook, flipped through pages and stopped. He looked up and said, "Tomorrow."

"Irony," said Hawkes. "The kid kills himself the day before his birthday."

"Ironic, but maybe not a coincidence. Adam Yunkin didn't want to see sixteen," said Stella.

"It could be nothing," said Mac.

"Could be everything," said Stella.

"Gun Hill area," said Mac. "While Hawkes is looking for an office decorator, see if you can talk to someone at the Gun Hill precinct who can give us a lead on an office being painted Vineland Green."

"I'm on it," said Flack. "I know a couple of people in that precinct."

Mac heard something behind him. He looked over his shoulder at the window. It had begun to rain again.

Anne Havel made the call and asked to talk to whoever was in charge of investigating her husband's murder. She was put through to Danny Messer.

While she waited, she glanced out the living room window, ignoring her father-in-law, Waclaw, who sat numbly on the sofa.

The days of rain had taken her through many moods. At first, before Alvin had been murdered, she had welcomed the protective wall of the deluge that isolated her from the world. Even as a child she had welcomed the heavy, driving rain.

After three days, the isolation had ceased to be comforting and had become confining. The house was not big; three small bedrooms, living room, dining room, kitchen. The rain kept the children home and Waclaw had sat watching television, even though he didn't understand most of it, from morning till night.

The house had become a confining trap. And now, with the cruel return of the rain, it had suddenly struck her as a good place to end her life.

"Detective Messer," said Danny.

"This is Anne Havel."

"What can I do for you, Mrs. Havel?"

So much, she thought. Take that zombie of a man away. Sit with her children day and night for at least a week. Make the rain stop. Make it stop.

"My husband left a diary," she said. "It's in Polish. He was having an affair with someone at the school."

"Who?"

"He didn't write the name, only called the person 'Nogi,' 'Legs' in Polish."

"We'll need that diary."

"It's yours," she said, hanging up the phone and turning to her father-in-law. "Are you hungry?"

If Waclaw understood, he gave no sign.

Anne walked to the kitchen. She would do the easiest thing possible. She would make peanut butter and jelly sandwiches. The girls would be fine with that. Waclaw wouldn't care.

She opened the refrigerator. No peanut butter.

Keith Yunkin sat in the comfortable, new office swivel chair. He had unpacked and assembled it the day before. It was the only piece of furniture in the office. The floor was polished wood and the walls freshly painted in what was supposed to be a restful green.

Other furniture would be moved in, possibly today. The office and the rest of the building, now that it was almost truly finished, would begin coming to life. Keith listened for the sound of movers and curious tenants. He would hear them coming down the hall when they started to come in. Now that the rain had begun to fall again they would almost certainly not be moving in today. Plenty of time to pick up his duffel bag, slide open the window and step out into the rain.

On his lap was a paper towel he had taken from a diner bathroom. On top of the towel was a half-finished sandwich, peanut butter and jelly. He was hungry. There was another sandwich in his duffle, an egg salad on rye. He would probably eat that too.

He couldn't stop thinking about Ellen Janecek. He had to complete the cycle. Everyone in the group would have to pay for Adam's death. He had chosen Sunderland's group randomly. It was a place to start, a symbolic place, a statement. After he had killed her, he would call the *Times*, the *Post*, the local news. He would tell them what he had done. He would give them details. Molesters would learn about the murders and live in terror thinking they might be next. Even if he was caught, they would sit behind locked doors in fear of someone else doing as he had done.

The boy that the blank-eyed pretty Ellen Janecek had seduced was almost two years younger than Adam when his brother died. Better to be seduced by a pretty young woman than raped by a bear-faced middle-aged man, if that could be considered a choice.

It would have been better if he had been able to complete the ritual within the twenty-four hours of the anniversary of his brother's death. But he could do it today. Lots of time today. He couldn't wait too long. He couldn't kill on his brother's birthday. That wasn't a day for revenge. It was a day to honor a short life.

He had to kill Ellen Janecek. The police would be watching, but he had to do it. His task was unfinished. He couldn't leave it that way. For the sake of Adam's memory, he couldn't leave it that way.

He didn't know what he would carve into her soft white flesh. He knew it would come to him at the moment he needed to know. He was inspired by his brother's memory, his parents' agony and his own rage. It would come to him, but first he had to find a way to get to Ellen Janecek.

• • •

French green clay is used for external cosmetic treatments by practitioners of alternative medicine. French green clay belongs to a subcategory of clay minerals known as illite clays. Rock quarries in southern France had a monopoly on its production till deposits were identified in China, Montana and Wyoming. The clay is green because it comes from a combination of iron oxides and decomposed plant matter, mostly kelp seaweed and other algae. Other components include montmorillonite, dolomite, magnesium, calcium, potassium, manganese, phosphorus, zinc, aluminum, silicon, copper, selenium and cobalt. Water removed. Clay sun-dried. French green clay stimulates skin and removes impurities from epidermis. Clay absorbs impurities from the skin cells, causes dead cells to slough off and stimulates flow of blood to epidermis. As clay dries on skin, it causes pores to tighten.

And that clay was what Lindsay found in one of the epidermal surface specimens taken from the people at the Wallen School.

French green clay, easily and inexpensively purchased at most health food stores, supposedly has curative powers when ingested. It is simply one kind of processed dirt, but Lindsay knew that people all over the world ate dirt, believed it was even a staple for health. The practice went back at least to medieval times.

In addition to being eaten, French green could be applied to the skin to bring up impurities. It might also bring up fragments of glass.

Lindsay needed a volunteer to spray glass fragments on and into his skin and then see if French green clay would pull the fragments out. There was only one readily available volunteer: Lindsay Monroe.

If it worked, she and Danny would have a suspect.

Stella got the call just before noon. She recognized the voice.

"I just talked to the arson investigator," Devlin said. "He confirmed what you found. Professionally placed explosives."

"Good," said Stella.

She was wearing her lab coat and gloves and sitting in front of a microscope examining a minute fragment of debris from the bomb site. Hawkes had gone to the DNA lab. He was now standing in the doorway, motioning to Stella.

She held up a hand, indicating that he should wait while she took the call.

"There's more," Devlin said. "Our investigator checked on the insurance. Doohan had a two-hundred-thousand-dollar policy on Doohan's. He could have sold the place for six times that much."

"Maybe he needed money fast," she said.

"An insurance company fast? He could have sold the bar today, cash, for four hundred thousand."

"It doesn't make sense," she said.

"No," said Devlin. "It doesn't. Unless your talkative man in with the broken ankle is lying to you."

Hawkes stood in the doorway, arms folded, looking at her.

"I should be hearing this from your arson investigator," Stella said.

"I asked him if I could make the call," said Devlin. "Ulterior motive. Dinner and a movie. You pick the movie. I pick the place we eat."

"When?" she asked.

"Tuesday or Sunday," he said. "My nights off."

"Two questions," she said.

"Sure."

"Are you married?"

"No. Never even been close. What else. My father was a fireman. So is my brother. I have a sister, lives in Teaneck, has three kids. I'm a practicing Catholic and will remain so till I get it right. I've been a fireman for seven years. Joined the day I finished college. NYU, pre-law. I'm a Yankees and Knicks fan. That's it. Life story."

"That could have waited," she said, looking at Hawkes who was yawning.

"Saves time," he said. "I don't mean it saves time so we can—"

"Understood," said Stella. "Devlin, I'm older than you by at least four years."

"How do you know?" he asked.

"I'm good at estimating ages. Part of my job, though I usually do it on dead people."

"It's part of your intrigue," he said with a laugh she liked. "I mean the age difference, not your working with the dead. I work with the dead a lot too. Gives us something in common."

"Dinner and morbid conversation?" she asked.

"Your life story?"

"Tuesday night maybe," she said. "I'll find a comedy, something with Will Ferrell or Owen Wilson."

"Sounds good. You like Greek food, right?"

"I like to eat," she said.

"Give me an address and I'll pick you up at seven."

"I'll pick a place and meet you there," she said.

"Deal," Devlin said.

She hung up and walked over to Hawkes.

"Houston," he said. "We've got a problem."

That was all he said on the walk down the hall to the DNA lab where Jane Parsons was waiting for them.

"Two of your building explosion victims are related," Jane said. "Identical twins, as you know, are the only people who have the exact same

DNA, but close relatives—siblings, parents, even first cousins—have enough markers to confirm a relationship."

"Enough to go to court with?" asked Stella.

"We could," said Jane, "but a decent defense attorney can always create doubt. So this is just for you."

"The cook, Malcom Cheswith," said Hawkes. "He's related to Connor Custus."

Jane nodded her agreement.

Stella was too weary to be stunned, but not too weary to be very curious.

"It's all relative," said Stella.

"What is?" asked Jane.

"That's what Custus said to me in the hospital. Said it three times. He was playing with me."

"Let's go talk to Custus," said Hawkes.

"Let's," said Stella.

As they headed for the door, deep thunder rolled outside and lightning cracked somewhere not far away and the rain came down.

Stella was confident that she would come up with the right questions for Custus. What she wasn't confident of was what she would wear on Tuesday night for her date with Devlin. That would depend on whether or not the rain stopped by then. Like so many others in the five boroughs, she was beginning to think that the deluge might not end for a long, long time.

• • •

To say that the pain was great would be unfair to the pain that was monumental, epic, even awe inspiring. He had felt pain many times before, a few which came close to this moment as he got out of the hospital bed.

The trick was to keep the weight, all weight, off his right ankle. No mean trick, but he was accustomed to performing tricks.

A greater trick would be to find something to wear. He could hardly escape from the hospital hopping on one leg in a white and blue striped gown that tied in the back and showed his sunny backside.

He had spun a tale, but the threads were thin and would no doubt be torn apart by the doctor named Hawkes and the detective named Stella.

Had he not broken his ankle and fallen into the darkling maw of the fetid earth, he would not have had to create the identity of Connor Custus. He, Charles Roland Cheswith, could have simply wandered off into the rain having pressed a button on his phone and disposed of his brother and Doohan. But Doohan had seen him. Doohan had run into the rain to stop him. Doohan's alibi wasn't in place.

Doohan's dentist had canceled all appointments. Besides, Doohan had second and third thoughts about the whole thing. The man with the Irish

accent who called himself Sean Hanlon had told
him that he had set up an insurance policy with
a Dutch company for Doohan's. Payoff price: one
million and two hundred thousand dollars. Doohan had bought the lie and signed his name to the
policy, which Charles Roland Cheswith planned
to let fall into the hands of the police. Poor Doohan had, they would conclude, bought the policy,
blown up his tavern and died in the effort, especially when Cheswith called the police to confess
that he had been hired by Doohan to blow up the
bar.

There should have been no connection made
between Charles and his brother, Malcom, the
cook who would cook no more, the brother who
had parlayed salary, a small inheritance from a
co-worker with no relatives and some remarkable
luck and skill at sports betting, into almost two
million dollars. The two million, of which Malcom
had proudly written his brother, was to be a down
payment on a very small restaurant in Soho.

Cheswith, well stoked with pain relievers, managed to stand.

Charles had learned his bomb-making skills
before he was twenty in Dublin. He had not been
particularly good at it. He had the scars to prove it.

At the age of twenty-five, he had taken to the
stage, had become an actor. Dinner theater in
Texas, Alabama, Louisiana. A rare, small part in a

television series episode, twice as a corpse. People would recognize him on the street but have no idea where they had seen him before. Perhaps the highlight of his long and unsuccessful career was his appearance on a network game show in which he won twenty-six thousand dollars.

Connor Custus had been a rather good improv character, especially considering the pain he had been in and the great likelihood of impending doom under water of such filth as to best not be thought of.

He had succeeded in his performance and failed in his plot. Now, to get away, Charles Cheswith would have to improvise as he never had before. He still had hopes. If he could get away, get back to Australia, wait to be contacted by lawyers about his brother's estate, he would be fine.

There was no police officer guarding his room. He was not a suicide threat and he could hardly move from his bed with a broken ankle and full of painkillers with nurses checking on him. But he would do it. The great disappointment would be that the performance he would now have to give might be seen by few and appreciated by none.

He almost fell as he took his first hop toward the door. He steadied himself on the night table. The plastic water pitcher fell over. The table quaked. Charles did not fall.

"Harder than playing Stanley Kowalski," he said, biting his lower lip.

Charles had never really played Kowalski. He had understudied the role in *A Streetcar Named Desire* when it was being played by a soap opera actor in a summer one-week run at a dinner theater in San Antonio.

Charles had eight thousand dollars in cash in the hotel where he was staying. He had a passport with his real name on it, an Irish passport. It was enough to get him out of the country.

Time for the next hop.

Hand against the wall, Charles made his way toward the door.

15

FLACK FOUND A VETERAN DETECTIVE in the precinct near the Gun Hill Road subway station. The detective, Stuart Bain, had been a friend of Don Flack's father.

"Buildings being painted," Bain said, standing outside the precinct under an eave where he could smoke without violating the law and getting wet from the rain. "How big a place we talkin' about here?"

"Don't know," said Flack.

"We've got a list we watch," said Bain. "Unoccupied places being built, remodeled. You wouldn't believe what people'll steal. One place they took new tile right off the floor at night while the glue was drying. I'll get you the list. But you know it might not be on there."

"I know," said Flack. "How's Scott?"

Bain finished his cigarette, fieldstripped it and said, "My son, Scott, is off fighting in Iraq. Was a time he considered becoming a rabbi. You know that?"

"Don't think so," said Flack.

"Now all he's considering is coming back alive and in one piece," said Bain. "Come on. I'll get you the list. I'll go with you. Check it out. Guy killed how many yesterday?"

"Four," said Flack.

"Maybe some backup wouldn't hurt," Bain said.

"Maybe it wouldn't," said Flack.

"Ellen?"

She wouldn't have taken any chances, not after she had been fooled the night before. The voice of the caller last night, the man she knew as Adam, wasn't really like Jeffrey's, but she had deluded herself. Not again. She was no fool.

"Jeffrey?"

She was alone in the hotel room. The room wasn't as nice as the one she had been in the night before. She had the feeling the police were punishing her for leading Adam to the hotel, for getting Paul killed.

The police had asked her to give them her phone. She had refused, said she needed it to stay in touch with her parents because her father was very ill, that she would tell the man in the bathroom if anyone called.

This call had come at the perfect moment. It was almost a sign. The officer, David McCord, had gone into the bathroom. The phone had rung. It was Jeffrey. No doubt. But she asked to be sure, to be reassured.

"Jeffrey, you sound—"

"I have to see you," he said. "Now. Soon."

He sounded like the sixteen-year-old boy he was, not the fourteen-year-old man-child she had first known and loved and wanted and needed.

"I'm sorry, Jeffrey. I can't. Not for a few days. Then we'll find a way to be together. I promise."

She had almost called him "baby." He didn't like that.

"I've got to," he said.

She heard the toilet flushing. Not much time. Seconds.

"I'll kill myself if I don't see you today," Jeffrey said, his voice definitely trembling.

"Gronten Hotel on Twenty-seventh Street," she said. "Room eight-eleven. Say you're my nephew. Tell them I told you to bring me something, a book. Pick up a book."

"I'm sorry," Jeffrey said.

"Don't be," she said.

This time she called him "baby."

"That was fine," said the limping man, taking the cell phone from the boy's hand and closing it. "You don't have to be afraid. I'm not going to hurt you."

"What're you showing me?" Danny asked.

Lindsay sat in front of him, palms up. The palms were almost beet red.

"Palms without glass fragments," she said.

He held out his hands and said, "Palms without glass fragments. What's your point?"

"I sprayed glass fragments into my palms," she said.

"Sounds like fun," Danny said. He grimaced.

"Then I applied French green clay like the clay I found on one of the palms of the people at Wallen we examined."

"And you found?"

"The clay didn't remove glass fragments. I had to pry them out."

"That had to hurt," said Danny.

"It didn't feel good. The interesting thing is I got the glass out, but I didn't get rid of all the green clay stain. Our killer did the same."

"So we have a suspect," said Danny. "Someone with a slightly green palm, swollen like yours where the fragments were removed."

"We have a suspect," Lindsay said with a smile.

"Wrong, Montana," Danny said. "We've got two suspects. I took another look at the videotape, sections that hadn't been altered."

"And you found?"

"I'll show you," he said.

It was Danny's turn to smile.

They moved down the hall to where Danny had set up the videotape.

"There," he said. "Students in Havel's ten o'clock class going into the lab."

He stopped the image on each of the four students.

"Got it so far?" he asked.

"Nothing to get yet," she said, standing behind him.

"Right," he agreed. "But now we go forty minutes after the class ended. I've isolated images of all the students. Annette Heights."

On the screen, frozen with a click, Annette Heights, the girl with the cute round face and wavy dark hair, was openmouthed, talking to two other girls.

"Okay," said Danny, pressing a button.

The images shot by and then stopped.

"Karen Reynolds," he said.

The tall girl was walking alone down a corridor toward the camera. Lindsay examined the image and nodded. Danny moved to the next image he had isolated.

"James Tuvekian."

The boy sat at a table in the cafeteria across from another boy. It was the same table where Danny had interviewed the students and faculty.

"And finally, Cynthia Parrish," he said.

The girl was standing next to a locker. A boy was leaning over her, one hand resting on the wall over her right shoulder. She was looking up at him. She looked as if she were about to cry.

"See it?" Danny asked.

"I see it," Lindsay said. "One of our kids changed clothes."

"And why would someone do that?"

"Blood," said Lindsay. "Get rid of the bloody clothes. Alter the tapes."

"Let's go talk to our suspects," said Danny.

"I'll get my kit."

"Bring an umbrella," Danny said.

He hadn't been able to get the bloody clothes she had been wearing out of the building. Too many eyes. The alarm had come too quickly. The damned queer O'Shea had found Havel's body too soon.

He had improvised, gotten the gym bag out of her locker, helped her change. It wasn't supposed to happen like this. Havel wasn't supposed to die. But it had happened and he had done his best to cover it up.

Now he had to dance just ahead of the two CSI detectives.

He was dancing as fast as he could.

If you were homeless, finding a reasonably or unreasonably dry place to get out of the rain was growing increasingly difficult. There were underpasses, but they were three inches deep with dark water. There were basements with broken windows, but they were minilakes with floating garbage. There were abandoned buildings, but they were thick with bottom-rung crack addicts or the clinically insane.

The Hat was in search of something better.

The Hat, of course, always wore a hat, whatever kind of hat he could find or filch. It was his trademark. It was all he really had to identify himself among the shaggy, skinny, toothless old men with unkempt hair and beards.

The Hat had another name. He hadn't forgotten it. He just had trouble attaching it to the creature of the streets he had become.

The Hat knew a place to get out of the rain, an office building that was almost finished. The Hat knew a window he could pry open. He would just have to keep watch for guards. There wouldn't be any contractors or builders or workers today, not with the rain.

All he needed was something to eat.

He wouldn't steal. No need. If you were willing to walk and knew where you were going, you could always get a free meal, a not-bad meal. You didn't even have to dig into the garbage bins down by the food court in Grand Central Station.

The Hat went through the window and almost lost the St. Louis Rams cap he was wearing. It tipped back when he went through the window, but it didn't fall off. He made a note to clean up the prints from the window before he left. The Hat closed the window behind him and stood quietly, sniffing the air.

Over the fumes of freshly painted office walls, he smelled peanut butter.

There wasn't much blood on the hospital blues that Charles Cheswith found in the hamper outside the open door of Room 203. A woman was mopping inside the room, speaking to someone in Spanish. Charles had been lucky. She was just across from the room in which he had been.

No one was looking down the corridor his way.

He might have found something cleaner, but he didn't have time to fish around. He took the blues and hobbled to a door marked "Custodial." The door was open. He clicked on the light and took off his hospital gown. The room smelled like solvent or cleaning fluid. Charles had always liked the smell of Lysol and gasoline. His brother, Malcom, had a more delicate sense of smell. There had never been much compatible between them.

The small room contained white plastic bottles, packages of napkins, bolts of toilet paper, paper towels. Charles needed a pair of shoes or slippers. He needed crutches. He needed to get the hell out of the hospital.

He opened the door a crack and peered out. The cleaning woman with the hamper had moved farther down the corridor. Charles came out and went into the room she had exited.

Two beds, both occupied. A skinny, gray man in need of a shave lay sleeping in the nearby bed. His mouth was open. He was snoring. In the other bed, a short broad man with black wavy hair that looked dyed looked up at Charles and said, "Que pasa?"

"Stubbed my toe," said Charles with a rueful smile. "Just now coming out of surgery."

"You should take care of that, Doctor," said the man.

"On my way to do just that," Charles said. "Just checking on the patient here."

Charles hobbled to the first bed and looked at the chart at the foot of the bed. Then he looked up.

"Fine," he said.

"He's gonna die," said the man in the far bed.

"We all are," said Charles.

"Pero este hombre va a morir hoy o manana."

"Que lastima," said Charles. "Tengo a tomar sus zapatos."

"Por que?"

"He won't be needing them anymore," said Charles, holding on to the bed and leaning over. A pair of hospital slippers were just under the bed. He managed to fish them out without falling.

"I guess not," said the man.

"Does he have crutches?"

"No," said the man, "but I do."

"Mind if I borrow them? I'll get another pair and send these right back."

Charles awkwardly managed to put on the slippers.

"I guess," said the man. "They're hospital crutches."

Charles hobbled to the man's bed. The crutches leaned against the wall near the head of the bed. Charles reached for them.

"You are one fuckin' bad liar," the man said, grabbing Charles's wrist.

Charles tried to pull away, but the man was remarkably strong.

"I thought I was pretty good at it," Charles said. "I'm just having a bad day."

The man let go of Charles's wrist and said, "So am I," said the man, "but you can bounce away. I can't."

The man patted the blanket where his right leg used to be.

"Diabetes," the man said.

"Sorry," said Charles, taking the crutches.

"You think you're having a bad day? Talk to me about bad days," said the man, turning away.

"We'd like to look in your locker," said Danny.

"My locker? What for?"

"We think you know," said Lindsay.

A tall, broad young uniformed officer named Dave Wolfson stood behind her. Wolfson had been drafted as a wide receiver by the Jets. He got cut early in the season and became a cop. He still played weekend football for the NYPD team. Wolfson knew how to smile. He just didn't do it when he was on the job.

"You'll need a warrant."

"We can get one," said Danny. "Officer Wolfson will just stand guard in front of your locker till it arrives."

"I want a lawyer."

"We haven't charged you with anything," said Lindsay. "Are we going to need that warrant?"

"No."

"Let's go," said Danny.

They went down the steps at the end of the main corridor in the Wallen School. Classes were in session. Footsteps of the quartet clicked down the stairs. They went into a room at the end of the lower level corridor. The room was just past the video security center where a woman in a security uniform looked up at them from the screens.

Danny, Lindsay and Wolfson moved to a quintet of lockers. The man inserted a key into the lock on the third locker and stood back. Danny opened the door. The locker was empty, clean.

"You cleaned it out?" asked Danny.

"Yesterday," he said.

"Then why didn't you want us to look inside it?" Danny asked.

"It's empty. I knew you'd ask me why."

"Why?" asked Danny.

"I took a few things, computer programs, a hard drive, some things. You going to turn me in?"

"You've got bigger worries," said Danny. He nodded at Lindsay. She set down her kit, reached into it and came up with a spray and a pair of goggles. The others stood and watched as she sent a mist onto the inside of the locker door. Dozens of fingerprints appeared. Lindsay put the spray back in the kit and came up with a pack of transparencies inside of clear plastic envelopes. She selected one and held it up to the locker door.

"Your fingerprints aren't inside this locker," she said.

"I don't understand. Maybe I never touch—"

"This isn't your locker," said Danny. "Which one is it? We can open them all."

Resigned, the man moved to the first locker and used another key on his chain to open it.

Officer Wolfson moved to the door of the small room. Danny reached over and opened the locker door. Inside, on the high shelf, were two books. Hanging on one of the three hooks was a shirt.

"Looks like blood," said Danny.

On the bottom of the locker was a white plastic grocery bag. Lindsay reached over, gloves on, and opened the bag.

"And what's this?" asked Danny.

He got no answer.

"More blood," said Lindsay, taking something carefully from the bag.

She held up a dress. The front of it was covered with dried blood splatter.

"Want to tell us who the girl is?" asked Danny.

"What girl? I found that in the garbage this morning. I was going to turn it in to you."

"You weren't in a big hurry," said Danny.

"I did it on my own."

"Did what?" asked Danny.

"Killed Havel."

"We'll see," said Lindsay.

"I want a lawyer now," said Bill Hexton.

"Now," Lindsay said, "you get one."

• • •

Keith Yunkin watched the bald man heading toward the door of the hotel with an older man who was talking animatedly. Both men held black umbrellas and the pounding rain made them raise their voices to be heard. The bald man was carrying a container of coffee in one hand, umbrella in the other, and a newspaper under his arm. He glanced at the hotel entrance, looking as if he wanted to escape.

"You can close the deal by dropping two points," said the older man as they made it up the stairs and under the alcove in front of the hotel entrance. "Two points, Jerry. You'll still walk away with what . . . ?"

"One hundred and forty-two thousand," said the bald man.

"One hundred and forty-two thousand," repeated the older man.

"One hundred and forty thousand is ten years ago's sixty thousand," said Jerry.

"So you're going to pass up writing the policy because of nostalgia? Insurance is insurance."

"That it is," said Jerry.

Keith stood to the side, listening.

"So you're going to write it up or not?" the older man said.

Jerry pressed a button on the umbrella to close it. He had purchased it from a one-eyed nervous vendor this morning for five dollars. It was work-ing just fine.

"I'll write it up," said Jerry. "When I get back to Dayton."

"Before you go home," pressed the older man. "Jerry, don't give me a heart attack here."

"Before I go home," Jerry conceded.

The older man patted Jerry's shoulder and grinned. He was getting a piece of the action and it was enough.

"Gotta go," said the older man. "You going up to your room and getting it done now, right?"

"Right."

"I'll send a messenger to pick it up in an hour, okay?"

"An hour's fine," said Jerry.

The older man looked at the sky and shook his head. He muttered, "Fucking rain," and ran to the curb where a cab was waiting.

Keith walked up to Jerry, doing his best to hide the limp he knew the police would be on the look-out for. They would also be looking for a lone man. He meant to remedy that situation right now.

"Jerry?" he said as the bald man turned to head for the hotel.

"Yeah."

"I thought it was you," Keith said, holding out his hand to shake. "Ted Wingate from Dayton. You sold my uncle a great policy on his business."

Jerry took the offered hand and said, "Frank Terhune?"

"My uncle," said Keith. "What brings you to New York?"

"Insurance," said Jerry. "You?"

"Surgery," said Keith. "Leg. Long, boring story. Afghanistan. Got a minute? I haven't talked to anyone from home in weeks."

Jerry hesitated and then said, "Sure. We can sit in the lobby or—"

"Mind if we go to my room? I've got to make a call."

"No, that'll be fine. I just have a few minutes."

"Me too. I've got a check up at Mount Sinai at one. Wait. They were just starting to clean my room when I came down."

"We can go to my room," said Jerry.

They walked in together. Keith put his hand on Jerry's arm to steady himself, hide the limp. The hand made Jerry uncomfortable, but he wasn't about to distance himself from a wounded veteran.

Installation art. That's what it looked like to The Hat. A long time ago. A year? Six years? He had been an artist. A real artist. Shows in galleries in San Antonio, Los Angeles, Dallas, Chicago, Manhattan. He could have designed something like this back then.

A cleanly painted room with shining floors. A single office chair in the middle. Someone sitting almost motionless. A boy in jeans and a blue pull-over shirt, short sleeves.

The Hat stood in the doorway, looking at the kid who looked back at him but didn't move.

"You okay, kid?" asked The Hat.

"I don't know."

The Hat stepped into the room. Nothing seemed to be holding the kid in the chair. He wasn't tied up. There was no bomb attached to him.

"Why are you sitting there?" asked The Hat. "You hungry?"

"No. He, this guy, told me to sit here till he got back," said the kid.

"Guy?"

"I don't know his name. He came for me at school, outside of school. Said Ellen was waiting for me."

"Ellen?" asked The Hat.

The truth was that Jeffrey was more frightened of this guy than he had been of the man with a limp. The man with the limp had talked to him softly, calmly, assured Jeffrey that he wouldn't be hurt, and Jeffrey believed him. Jeffrey also believed him when he said he would be very sorry if he got out of the chair before the man got back.

Jeffrey didn't feel the same about this guy. He knew homeless when he saw it.

"She wasn't waiting for you? This Ellen," said The Hat.

"No. He called her. I think he wants to kill her. He's got a knife."

The Hat knew kids this age who drank, smoked, snorted, ate and shot up with all kinds of crap that had them seeing murder where there was none. This kid was none too bright, but he looked clean.

"Kid, just get up and go home," said The Hat. "You got money?"

"No," Jeffrey said warily. "But I have a Metrocard."

The Hat moved to the middle of the room to help the boy up, but the boy didn't need help. There was nothing wrong with him.

"Maybe I better just wait," Jeffrey said.

"Maybe you better just get the hell out of here," said The Hat.

"Hold it," came a voice behind them.

The Hat froze, then turned around.

Don Flack stood in the doorway, gun in hand. The Hat knew he was a cop. He looked cop, probably smelled cop if they got close to him.

"I just came in to get out of the wet," The Hat said.

He looked harmless, but Flack knew better than to count on that.

"Keep your hands where I can see them," he said, taking a step into the room.

The Hat held his hands out. So did the boy.

"The man with the limp," said Flack. "Where is he?"

"Left," said Jeffrey.

"Who are you?" asked Flack.

"Jeffrey Herdez."

The name rang bells, lots of bells.

"Ellen Janecek," said Flack.

"He's going to hurt her," said the boy. "He said it was because of what she did to me. Ellen didn't do anything to me."

The Hat was lost. "The rain," he said. "We just—"

"You see the man?" asked Flack, putting his gun back in the holster under his jacket but keeping his distance.

"No," said The Hat.

Flack took out his phone, flicked it on, pushed a speed dial button, waited a beat and said, "Mac. Yunkin's on the way to the hotel to get Ellen Janecek. Might be there by now."

A pause. "You are?" said Flack into the phone. "Right. I'll get him home."

Flack turned the phone off and looked at the homeless man.

"Let yourself out the way you came in," he said.

The Hat didn't need to be told twice.

16

"LEGS," SAID DANNY.

They were sitting in the conference room next to the headmaster's office. Marvin Brightman, the headmaster, was at one end of the table, hands folded, wondering if he would be updating his résumé in the next week.

Danny sat at the other end of the table. Bill Hexton was across from him. They were waiting for a lawyer. It might be a long wait. John Rothwell, the lawyer who represented the Wallen School, had been called, but his firm backed off. Said it would be a possible conflict of interest if the police were planning to arrest one of the Wallen School students in connection with the investigation. They had recommended another firm.

The return of the throbbing downpour would definitely delay the arrival of the attorney.

"Legs," Danny repeated. "Havel kept a journal. Said he was involved with a student he called 'Legs.'"

Hexton looked at him, impassive, resigned, determined.

"You said you did it on your own," said Danny. "That wasn't true."

The headmaster shifted uncomfortably but didn't speak. Hexton didn't answer.

"We know whose dress that was in your locker," said Danny. "Size fits only one of the girls in that chem class and the video confirms which one. My partner's talking to her right now."

Nothing from Hexton.

"You hid in the chem closet before class," said Danny. "Plan was to come out when the students left. Plan was to warn Havel to leave her alone, maybe even push him around a little, maybe push him around a lot, but you heard noise. When you came out Havel was facedown on the desk, pencil in his neck. She was standing over him covered in blood. She had her uniform on under her dress. She took the dress off. You got her cleaned up and then you took another pencil and drove it into his eye. He was already dead. You wanted to take responsibility for killing him if you got caught. One big problem. You want to know what it was?"

"No," said Hexton.

"I do," said Brightman.

"Blood splatter," said Danny. "The blood on the dress shows that whoever wore it struck the first, the fatal blow. You going to claim you were wearing the dress?"

No answer.

"Okay," Danny went on. "No blood splatter from the second blow, the one to the eye. No splatter on your uniform. The blood had stopped pulsing in Havel's body. He was dead. No splatter. You drove a pencil into the eye of a dead man to make it look as if you had struck both blows. Angle's wrong. Splatter's wrong. And we believe there was glass in your palm from using the jar. You tried to use green clay to get the glass out, but you had to dig the glass out yourself. And your palm is still slightly green."

Hexton looked as if he were going to speak, but Danny stopped him.

"You'd better wait for your lawyer. There'll be an assistant DA here soon. The two lawyers can talk to each other. I'm finished," said Danny.

"Detective, I've advised Miss Reynolds not to say anything," said John Rothwell, the Wallen School lawyer.

"I want to tell her," said Karen Reynolds of the golden hair and long legs.

"This won't be admissible," said Rothwell.

"She's eighteen," said Lindsay, turning on the small tape recorder.

They were in the headmaster's office. Beyond the door Karen Reynolds kept glancing toward where Danny was sitting with Bill Hexton and Marvin Brightman.

"I didn't mean to kill him," Karen said to Lindsay. "I knew Bill was in the closet, yes. The plan was for him to come out, face Mr. Havel, warn him. I went back into the lab when the others left. I told him to stop bothering me, calling me, touching me. We'd only done it once, two months ago. I was seventeen then. I told him I'd tell, that his wife would find out, the school would find out. He didn't care. Said no one would believe me. He grabbed me. I picked up the pencil and . . . I panicked. I didn't plan to kill him. I didn't. I wouldn't have stabbed him if he hadn't grabbed me."

"That's it," said Rothwell. "Not another word."

Lindsay reached over and turned off the tape recorder. She had enough.

Charles Roland Cheswith was a resourceful man and, if he had to say so himself, which he did, a very good actor. He never had the looks, the charisma of a leading man, but that was fine with him. Leading men get old, hang on, give up and start to compete, usually unsuccessfully, for character roles with Charles Cheswith, who already fit comfortably into the roles of father, priest, lawyer, pharmacist and cop. He could go back to the stage, although it would have to be far away and under a different name.

He still harbored a glimmer of hope that he could claim the substantial insurance on his brother, Malcom. It was not a great hope, but there were still possibilities to explore.

First things first, however.

He had a checklist. Not one he had written. He didn't need to write it. Charles had an outstanding memory cultivated by exercises and tricks collected from years of learning roles. He had once, not too long ago, played Murray the Cop in a production of *The Odd Couple* on a riverboat in Natchez. He had understudied all of the male roles and had been not only prepared to step in but eager to do so. He got his chance one Saturday performance when one of the actors fell suddenly ill with violent vomiting. Ipecac induced. For one performance, Charles got to play Oscar Madison.

Now Charles sat in a wheelchair at JFK Airport, passport and e-ticket in hand, waiting to board his flight to Vancouver. He knew places to get lost in Vancouver, places where he could heal and hide. He had the money from Doohan. It would carry him while he figured out a way to claim the insurance money.

He wasn't quite home free, but he was getting closer.

With the help of the crutches he had made it to the front of the hospital and into a cab, which had just pulled up. There were people ahead of him in line, but with crutches and bloody blue surgical garb he had pushed his way past them filled with apologies as he uttered, "Emergency. Sorry."

And they believed him, believed he was a doctor. It was one of his better performances. It had to be.

They would be able to track him to the cab he had taken. Of this Charles had no doubt. The pretty woman detective wouldn't give up or slow down. She had been relentless in rescuing him and her partner and figuring out what Charles had done. She would be relentless in tracking him.

But he had made it back to the hotel where he had a room. The front desk clerk glanced at the bloody blues, the crutches, the bandaged leg and said nothing. He got Charles's passport and cash from the hotel safe. Charles paid his bill, went to his room, changed his clothes in agonizing pain, and made his way back to the front of the hotel where he caught another cab.

All he had was a carry-on. No checking of luggage. In a washroom, Charles put on a pair of glasses, combed his hair forward and let his lower lip puff in a pout that announced that this character was not of high intellect.

A lean black man with a trim beard and a blue blazer and tie hurried him through security in a wheelchair. Charles had checked the departure board briefly, saw that the Vancouver flight was leaving in thirty-five minutes. He had purchased a one-way ticket. Charles knew Vancouver, had been in three episodes of *The A-Team*, two of *21 Jump Street* and four pilots for shows that didn't go anywhere. That had been a long time ago, but he still knew people there. One of them would put him up. He would tell them tales, lies and partial truths till he healed. He would lose weight, grow a mustache, change the color of his hair, become someone different, buy an illegal Canadian passport. It could and would work out. Charles Cheswith was a resourceful man.

He got the man who was pushing the wheelchair to stop at a mall shop where he bought a Mets cap, a pair of sunglasses and a magazine. He was ready, at the front of the line, early boarding for the man who needed assistance.

Then he saw them. He wasn't sure at first that it was Detective Stella Bonasera and Dr. Hawkes. He had to take off the sunglasses to be certain, but there they were, heading toward him through the crowd.

It was almost certainly over. He had run out of all but one option and that was more a dramatic gesture than a sincere probability. Still it was a possibility. He reached into his carry-on, took out a small bottle filled with almost clear liquid, removed his watch from his wrist and fumbled for a small length of twisted wire.

When Stella and Hawkes were standing in front of the wheelchair, Charles was ready. He looked up at them and said, "How did you find me so damned fast? No, hold that explanation."

"It's over," said Stella.

"I was just thinking that myself," Charles said. "But I'll try this just the same."

He pulled down the blanket in his lap to reveal a small bottle wrapped in thin wires. The wires were attached to a wristwatch.

"I'd like to leave now," he said.

No one around them seemed to notice.

"I'm sure you would," said Stella.

"It's not going to happen," said Hawkes.

"What have I got to lose?" asked Charles. "Do you really want to take a chance?"

"No chance," said Hawkes. "That's not a bomb. It's shampoo."

"You're sure?" said Charles. "You willing to risk innocent lives?"

"No risk," said Hawkes.

Stella stepped forward and took the wired shampoo bottle and attached watch from his hand.

"This is the way the world ends," said Charles, shaking his head.

"Not with a bang but a whimper," Hawkes supplied.

"I don't know if I'm insurable," Keith said as he and Jerry walked across the lobby of the Gronten Hotel toward the elevator.

There were six people in the small lobby. One of them, the one with his hands folded over a paperback novel in his lap, was definitely a cop. The cop looked a little weary, but he was doing his job. Keith could sense the man looking at him and the insurance salesman from Dayton as they stepped into the elevator. There would be another cop outside of Ellen's room. He would deal with that.

"Everybody's insurable," said Jerry as the doors closed. "The only question is, how much will it cost and is it worth it?"

Keith was blessed with great peripheral vision. He was looking at Jerry and nodding as if the salesman had just said something profound, but Keith could also see the cop in the chair looking in his direction.

They were the only ones on the elevator. Jerry pushed the button for the sixth floor. Close enough. Keith would have only two flights up to get to Ellen Janecek.

"Your leg, right?" asked Jerry as they rose.

"My leg," Keith agreed. "Army's covering treatment but what about complications down the line? My mother, Dotty, you know her?"

"Don't think so," said Jerry.

"She died last year. Left me financially but not physically comfortable."

The elevator doors opened.

"Let's see what we can come up with," said Jerry with a smile.

Room service. Coffee. Toasted bagels and cream cheese and within fifteen minutes Jerry was preparing a policy. He couldn't believe how easy it had been to sell it. It was a good policy, but it wasn't cheap. When he finished making changes, he passed the four-page document across the small table to Keith who signed and initialed in all the right places.

Keith looked at his watch.

"I've got to go down to my room for a few minutes. I'll be right back with a check."

"Fine," said Jerry. "I'll just call my office and get the paperwork rolling."

Keith went to the door as Jerry picked up his cell phone and pressed a button.

Keith liked him. After he killed Ellen Janecek, he could come back and talk to him for a while, get him to accompany Keith out of the hotel. That was the plan in any case. He hoped he would not have to kill Jerry.

• • •

Ellen waited.

She wanted, needed to see Jeffrey. The television was on. The sound was off. She didn't want to miss the knock she was expecting on the door.

He would be coming soon.

The room was small. Two uncomfortable chairs with arms. A bed. The television. A single window with a mesh screen and beyond it a view of a dirty brick wall. Bathroom. Long dark lightning-shaped crack on the tile floor. The other hotel had been better, but he, the one she knew as Adam, had found her there. Yes, it was partly her fault. No, it was completely her fault, but "fault" wasn't quite the right word. It was her responsibility, and the consequence of her decision to tell him where she was had led to this small room.

But it was going to change.

And it was going to change now.

The knock at the door was gentle. Two raps. Ellen stood.

Keith stood in the hall. He was ready. He was lucky. There was no cop in the hall. In a few seconds, this part would be over. The circle would be complete. The letters of his brother's name would be carved in bloody gashes. A-D-A-M. This time all four letters in her soft, white flesh. Their bodies, what he had left of them, would forever be the reminder of Adam's death and their own unclean actions.

The world was a shitty place. There were decent, innocent people born into it, people like Adam. They were defiled.

Keith's hand was in his pocket touching the cool metal handle of the knife. She would open the door. An instant of recognition on her pretty, vacant face and then click, jab under her arm, push her back, close the door, take his time, but not too much time.

He knocked again.

The door started to open.

Knife out. No one in the narrow corridor.

The door swung open.

Mac had heard the knocking at the door. He had sent the officer in street clothes guarding the corridor down to the lobby. Mac came out of the bathroom, moved past Ellen Janecek, who he motioned to back away. More knocking. Flack had called him less than half an hour ago. Mac had arrived at the hotel fifteen minutes later.

When he had quickly told Ellen what he planned to do, her only question was, "Is Jeffrey all right?"

Mac, gun in his right hand, reached out for the door with his left, and threw the door open.

Keith stood there, knife in hand.

"Drop the knife," Mac said gently, both hands on the gun now.

Keith looked over the shoulder of the man in

front of him, the man with the gentle, firm voice
and the gun. Keith could see Ellen Janecek's face
across the room. He wanted to tell the man with
the gun that he had to kill her, that he couldn't
leave this unfinished. He had a feeling that the
man with the gun would understand, but he also
had the feeling that the man with the gun would
shoot.

"You don't understand," Keith said calmly. "She
killed my brother. They all killed or destroyed
my brother and other brothers, sisters, children,
grandchildren. You have to understand."

Keith took a step forward, knife still in his hand.
Mac could feel the man's pain, a horrible frustration. Mac took a step back and said, "Put it down
now."

Keith tightened his grip on the knife. Maybe,
just maybe he could surprise the man with the
gun, make a move, stab him under the arm, make
him drop that gun.

"Don't," said Mac.

"There are a lot of animals out there who don't
deserve to live."

"Maybe," said Mac, taking a step forward. "I'm
not one of them. I talked to your mother. She
wants to hear from you."

Keith had few options left. He considered them.

"What's your name?" Keith asked.

"Taylor, Mac Taylor."

Keith looked at Ellen Janecek and tightened his grip on the knife. Before he had lost his leg he could have leapt across the room and gutted her before he was shot. That was before he lost his leg.

"Keith?"

Keith Yunkin nodded and dropped the knife.

The Hat walked under the elevated train tracks, clinging to the duffle bag that he had taken from the office building. He considered the theft of the bag a major triumph. The Hat had stood across the street from the office building, hidden in a doorway, until the cop came out with the kid.

Then he'd raced back into the office building and found the duffle bag in the room behind the one in which he'd found the kid. The bag had been tucked away under a sink. The Hat had grabbed the bag and fled the building.

Then, under the tracks and station above them, he had walked.

Now he stopped, looked around furtively, put the bag on the ground and leaned over to unzip it.

Knives. He could sell them somewhere. Clothes. Maybe they fit. An egg salad sandwich and bottles of water. He sat on a low block of concrete and ate.

The Hat reached into the bag and came up with one of the knives. He opened it easily and as he did the blade ran across his finger. He dropped his sandwich. The cut was deep, very deep, to the bone. The blade of the knife was bloody.

He'd have to find some bandages somewhere. A knife like this one could kill someone without a blink.

He let the knife tumble back into the bag, took out a shirt, wrapped it around his hand and gave serious thought to going to a drug store, but not for Band-Aids, for something much bigger than a Band-Aid. There was a clinic about six blocks away, but it was far and The Hat was bleeding. No, a drug store it would be. Maybe he could trade a knife for bandages.

It had begun as a very good day, The Hat thought. A good deed for a soft-brained boy had brought him a promising bag full of jangling goodies and a sandwich. It could turn into a bad day with a dark ending if the bleeding were not stopped. Oh well. The Hat knew people, lots of street people, who would be glad to buy these very sharp knives. But first, the bleeding had to stop.

Every drawer was occupied by a corpse. Nine of them. Sid Hammerbeck had been busy, nonstop for three days. Now he was home meditating in his state-of-the-art kitchen, amid shining pots, dark cast-iron pans, the smell of fresh vegetables and baking turbot. He took a spray of fresh chervil from a small paper bag in the refrigerator, placed it on a cutting board and expertly cut it into tiny, even pieces.

The timer was on. Sixteen minutes more.

It struck him that his life was one of smells, the smell of the dead, the smell of his own cooking. Sometimes he had guests over for dinner, but not tonight. Tonight he would dine alone. No conversation. No television. No book or newspaper on the table. He would eat slowly, close his eyes to savor the food without having someone across the table look at him as if he were doing something weird. His friends already thought his decision to leave the kitchen of one of the finest Continental restaurants in the city to go into the steel gray of the autopsy room was was weird enough.

Sid had explained that the room where he dissected the dead was cleaner than almost any four-star restaurant in the world. He could see disbelief, even when they said the obligatory and sophisticated "I know." Sid didn't explain much or often anymore.

Something itched, not physically, mentally. It was like trying to remember the name of a character in a favorite novel. There were several ways of dealing with it. Go back to the novel and find the name. Use some trick of the memory to locate the source of the itch and scratch it.

The microwave ticked behind him. Sid checked

the oven timer. Perfect. Turbot in the oven. Chive and crushed cauliflower in the microwave. An inexpensive California white wine barely chilling in the refrigerator.

What was bothering him?

One of the bodies.

He stood over the sink holding the garlic press in his hand. Patricia Mycrant. It came to him suddenly. Not words, but a faint smell wafting in the alcoholic miasma of the autopsy room and then a vision.

Three minutes to go. He would wait, take the fish from the oven, put the chervil and garlic away, refrigerate the cauliflower and chives and have a late dinner, maybe a very late dinner.

The wine would be too cold. He removed it from the refrigerator and placed it on the counter.

Twenty minutes later he was back among the dead.

Flack knocked at her door.

Less than an hour ago he had been lying on his sofa, shoes off, fully clothed watching a Rockies/Cubs game. He wasn't much interested in either team, but it was better than no game and it distracted him from the discomfort in his chest. He knew he couldn't concentrate on a movie or a series or read a book. He was hurting. He admitted it to himself, but no one else. He had come back from the trauma and surgery with rehab and rest, but on long days like this one, the aching, particularly in his chest, jarred him into memory.

When his phone rang, he was lying motionlessly, right arm across his eyes. He should get up and eat, maybe take a shower or bath, get some sleep, probably on the floor rather than his bed after taking one of his pain pills. It felt better to be on his back on the floor, though getting up in the morning was a series of challenges and pain.

The phone call had gotten him up and moving. Distraction was almost as good as sleep.

He knocked at the door again.

"Who is there?" came the voice.

"Detective Flack," he said.

"I'm not prepared for visitors," she said. "I've just bathed."

"Police business," he said.

Gladys Mycrant opened the door. She was wearing a black silk robe with colorful red and yellow flowers. Her hair was down and she wore makeup. Flack wondered if the makeup might be the tattooed kind.

"Yes?" she said, examining him and making it clear from her look that he came up short in her estimation.

"May I come in?"

"If you must."

She stepped back, hand holding her robe closed

at the breast. He entered and she closed the door.

"When am I getting Patricia's body?" she said. "I want to give her a decent burial. It's awful to think of her, the way she is, in some cold police mausoleum.

"The medical examiner had to complete another examination and run some tests."

"Tests?"

She sat in an armchair, legs crossed, bouncing impatiently.

"According to the medical examiner, your daughter's body is slightly yellow."

"Jaundice. Patricia drank. I told her what it would do to her liver, what it had done to her father's liver. Detective, I have a vivid imagination that helps me in my business but hampers me in my thoughts. I'd rather not think of my daughter as she is now."

"She was being poisoned," said Flack, looking down at her.

He didn't want to sit. His back told him not to. She was watching him. He knew she would see him wince, even if it were slight, when he tried to get out of a chair.

"Poisoned?"

"Arsenic," said Flack. "The ME found it in her nails, skin."

"ME?"

"Medical examiner."

"Oh my God," she said. "Something in the water? The walls? Am I poisoned too?"

"I doubt it, but we can check. She was dying from chronic arsenic poisoning," he said. "Slow."

She was silent now, biting her lower lip, thinking.

"You have plants?"

"Plants? In the house? No."

"You do on the roof."

"Yes."

"We'll check the soil for arsenic."

"She spent too much time with those plants, tending them. I shouldn't have—"

"You told me she didn't like to go on the roof, remember?"

"Did I? Yes, that's true, but she did enjoy the plants."

"We'll check your supplies for prints. You have arsenic?"

"No," she said indignantly. "Why would I have arsenic?"

"It's used for plant care," he said. "Mind if we look at your supplies?"

"I don't—"

"Gladys," he said gently. "Enough."

Her head was down. She wept into her silk robe.

"Patricia didn't die from arsenic poisoning," she said. "She was murdered by that maniac."

"But you were killing her slowly."

She nodded.

"She hadn't changed, wasn't changing. That group was doing nothing for her. I could tell by what she said, watched, listened to, the way she looked at children on the street. Bad genes. I've always attributed it to bad genes from her father's side. Nothing you can do to help someone with bad genes."

"So you were killing her."

"Softly," she said looking up. "Very softly. She was my daughter. But I didn't kill her, did I?"

"No."

"So you can't arrest me."

"The district attorney's office says that I can. I'm calling it attempted murder for the record, but they can straighten it out when you get there."

He read her her rights and told her he would wait while she dressed and called a lawyer. Gladys got out of the chair slowly and looked at him.

"You understand, don't you? You understand why I had to do it?"

"Doesn't matter what I understand," he said, but that was a lie. It mattered to Flack. It mattered very much.

17

Three Days Later

DEXTER THE UMBRELLA MAN was now Dexter the
Sunblock and Sunglasses Man. It hadn't rained in
three days. He was a man who moved with the
tides and the weather. He set up his table on Sixth
Avenue, a block from Rockefeller Center in front
of a McDonald's. Well, not right in front, but a few
feet to the side.

The table folded with two quick moves and became a box with a handle. The box was filled with
#45 Sol Ray Lotion whose label said it was made in
Brazil, and with Protecto-Vision Sun Glasses, dark
wrap-arounds with little stickers on the side that
also read "Made in Brazil."

Both products, Dexter knew, were made in St. Paul, Minnesota.

Business wasn't bad.

He kept watching the sky. No clouds. If it rained, he was prepared to fold up his box and go into McDonald's and eat dollar burgers and Cokes till it passed. Dexter was not going to duck under any awnings, not again, not ever. You never knew what might come through an awning.

Waclaw Havel finished packing.

He had made it through his son's funeral, held the hands of his grandchildren, comforted his daughter-in-law and grieved with them and the friends who had shown up at the church and the grave site.

The night before they buried Alvin, Waclaw had worried that the ground would be too wet, that they would be up to their ankles in mud and water and that the coffin would be lowered into a pond.

But it had been reasonably dry. No one had mentioned what had happened to Alvin. No one would mention what Alvin had done to bring it on himself.

The children would grow up. They would find out, but maybe not until they were adults or nearly so.

Anne was going to move as soon as she sold

the house, move back to Milwaukee where her parents and family lived and where she had grown up. No one from Anne's family had come to New York for the funeral. No one in Milwaukee wanted any connection to the man who had married Anne and brought shame and headlines in the *New York Post*.

Waclaw pushed the latch of his one suitcase and checked to see that it wasn't loose. Anne and the children were driving him to JFK. He would be back in Poland the next day. In Poland they would know nothing of Alvin's death and he planned to tell them a lie about that. Alvin will have met a terrible fate at the hands of a thwarted thief on the streets of the mythical and dangerous city.

"Ready?" asked Anne, standing in the doorway. Waclaw nodded.

"You can stay. You don't have to leave. You understand?"

He understood. There was nowhere to stay. He would be part of the past for her, for the children. He could not go with them to Milwaukee. He didn't want to go there.

He shook his head. He was ready.

Anne had given him photographs for his wallet, photographs of the children, herself and Alvin. He smiled. He smiled because he knew what he would remember, knew the tale he would tell to his family. He would tell them of the rain. He would tell them how he had floated on his back on a river. He would tell them how he had been rescued by a wild man wearing a plastic garbage bag.

They might even believe him.

Ellen Janecek was grateful. She really was. They had stopped Keith Yunkin. They had rescued Jeffrey. The sun was shining. She was grateful, but she wasn't happy. They wouldn't let her see Jeffrey. They didn't understand. Paul Sunderland had understood. It was simple, but every time she explained it to almost anyone she was met with patient or exasperated looks that made it clear they thought she was either a criminal or a crackpot.

Mac Taylor had told her that Jeffrey and his family were moving out of New York and that there was a court order for her to stay away from them. They had given Ellen court orders before. She had ignored them. They didn't understand. She was hurting no one. There was no victim. She would find him.

Jeffrey's mother had a younger sister who headed maid services at a big hotel in St. Louis. The sister offered Jeffrey's mother a job at almost twice the pay she was now getting. An apartment was also available at half of what she was now paying. St. Louis sounded good to her.

It didn't sound good to Jeffrey. He would be half a continent away from Ellen. He would move with his mother. He would enroll in school. He would do whatever he was supposed to do, even get an after-school job. He would do it till he had enough money saved and whatever he could steal from his mother's purse to get back to New York.

The law was stupid, but Jeffrey had learned that he could not argue with a law that said he should not be with a beautiful, smart woman who wanted him.

Ellen looked out of her apartment window, a cup of coffee in her hand. She smiled, cupping the coffee in two hands, looking at the flower shop across the street.

Stella almost didn't recognize him.

The bar was crowded, noisy. Devlin had again volunteered to pick her up at her apartment. Stella had again said she would meet him. No men in her apartment. Not yet. Maybe not ever. She had more than bad memories of the last man who had been with her in that apartment. He had attacked her, tried to rape and kill her, but it was she who had killed him. She should have moved, but Stella was determined not to be driven out by memories. However, no men in or near the apartment.

He was sitting at a very tiny round table in the rear of the crowded bar. She saw him looking at her. He cleaned up remarkably well. She had thought he was handsome in his uniform and soot-covered face. Across the room, smiling at her, he had calendar looks.

She made her way through the crowd, avoiding hands holding glasses, bodies leaning over to whisper and listen. She was wearing one of her two all-purpose black dresses. No come on. No keep your distance. This would be drinks, talk, that's it.

"Right on time," Devlin said, standing to greet her.

She smiled and sat down across from him. He motioned for a waitress who, in spite of the crowd, responded immediately and started for the table. Devlin was, Stella could see, the kind of man to whom waitresses paid attention.

The waitress stood next to the table. Devlin looked at Stella, who said, "Amstel Light."

The waitress looked at Devlin, who held up his empty glass. She nodded, smiled and began to navigate her way back to the bar.

"You look great," he said, having to lean forward to be heard.

"You too. We both look great. Now to the hard part," Stella said. "What, if anything, do we have in common?"

"I save lives," he said. "You find people who take lives."

"That's a start," she said. "What do you know about me besides that I look good in a black dress?"

"You're smart."

"And?"

"You've seen some bad things."

"How can you tell?" she asked.

"I see the same look in my eyes when I stand in front of the mirror at night and in the morning. What do you know about me?" Devlin asked.

"You don't want me to know how you hurt your wrist."

"You can't see my wrist," he said, tugging self-consciously at his right sleeve.

"I can see how you're holding your hand and I saw your wrist when you lifted your glass."

"Fire last night," he said. "A woman bit my wrist when I pulled her out of a burning room. Teeth marks still show. What else?"

"You don't usually dress like this, jacket, tie. The jacket has a white powder residue on the left shoulder. You've had it in a storage bag for a long time. And the tie is either the only one you own, your favorite tie or your lucky tie, or all three. It doesn't match the jacket and slacks and you'd be especially careful to make it match tonight if you could."

"So?"

"You want to impress me," she said. "I'm impressed."

"So am I. You always do this Sherlock Holmes business with men on a first date?"

"It's what I do all day long," she said. "Can't help it. Comes with the job."

The waitress delivered the beer for Stella and a fresh mug for Devlin.

"Anything else?" the waitress asked, looking at Devlin.

"Not now," he said. "Thanks."

The waitress left. Devlin held up his glass. Stella did the same with her Amstel. Glass and bottle clinked and Devlin looked up and shook his head.

"You all right?" asked Stella.

He reached into his pocket and came up with a cell phone. He cupped his left ear and held the phone up to his right ear.

"Yeah? What about Walt? No. It's okay." He looked at Stella. "I'll be there. Just roll."

He put the phone back in his pocket.

"Fire at St. Andrew's Church," he said. "I'm not supposed to be on tonight, but the other senior is sick. Sorry."

"I understand," said Stella.

And she did. The cell phone in the purse slung over her shoulder was set on vibrate. It had been pulsing for the past minute.

He stood.

"Go on," she said. "We'll give tonight a rain check."

"No more rain," he said. "A heat check maybe."

He leaned over, touched her hand and kissed her gently on the cheek.

"I'll call," he said.

"I'll answer," she said with a smile.

He left and Stella took out her own cell phone and saw that it was Hawkes who had called. She punched the right button and he answered.

"Hawkes, what's up?"

"Cheswith, the actor. He hanged himself. I was going to wait till tomorrow to tell you but—"

"No," she said. "That's fine."

"I liked the guy," admitted Hawkes.

"I know," she said. "So did I. Crime scene?"

"Holding cell. I'm on it."

"You want me to meet you there?"

"No," he said. "I'll take it. I just thought you'd want to know."

He hung up. So did she. The waitress came with the check. Stella paid it.

Danny missed a layup. He missed because he had been fouled by someone named Jorge who hit Danny in the face, knocking off his sports glasses. Danny got up and said, "Foul." It was a pickup game, five on five at St. Paul's gym. You called your own fouls. Your team held the court as long as it kept winning the eleven-basket game.

"Bullshit," said Jorge.

They were in each other's faces now. Jorge's

team was afraid of Jorge, who had a temper. Danny had seen the temper explode before. He didn't like playing against or with Jorge.

"No fuckin' foul, pussy," said Jorge.

Danny's teammates, including his friend Vince, who played like a lunatic, moved in to back Danny.

Danny was in a very dark mood. He had arrested Karen Reynolds. No, he and Lindsay had arrested her. The tall, blond young woman with great strong legs and an air of confidence had suddenly turned into a frightened girl. She had started to fall. Lindsay had caught her.

Karen Reynolds had looked up at both of them, tears streaming, face red.

"I didn't mean . . . He touched me. . . . Really, I tried to tell him. . . . I knew Bill was in the closet. . . . I tried to tell Mr. Havel, tell him to leave me alone. . . . He said he'd think about it. . . . Think about it . . . I . . . He grabbed me. . . . There in the classroom . . . I just . . . I did it. Please . . . my mother . . ."

Danny had wanted to help, but there was nothing he could do. It wasn't his job to help people who committed murder. He had done his job and done it well, but he still felt frustrated, darkened. And now Jorge was in his face, Jorge, under whose fingernails were small but clear traces of cocaine. Jorge was bigger than Danny. Jorge had a weightlifter's body. Jorge was angry with the world and ready for battle.

"Back off or get busted," said Danny.

"What? You a cop?"

"I'm a cop and you've got coke under your nails."

Jorge turned his head to one side and looked at Danny to see if he was bluffing. He could see that he wasn't. Jorge took a step back and pointed a finger at Danny, a finger that said "Next time it won't end like this."

"Shooting foul," said Danny. "I get a free one at the line."

Jorge nodded in temporary defeat. Both teams stepped back. The confrontation had taken less than a minute. Danny went to the line, thinking of the crying girl whose lawyers would claim self-defense. She might get off. Maybe she should. Either way her life was changed now and forever and she was only eighteen. The security guard, Bill Hexton, on the other hand, wouldn't get off. He had covered up a crime. He would lose his job. He would face jail time. The district attorney's office and a judge would decide how much.

Players from both teams lined up on the sides of the lane, hands up. Danny took the shot and missed. Jorge got the rebound and grinned.

All was not right with the world for Danny Messer this night.

• • •

Mac sat on the cot next to Keith Yunkin in the small, clean cell. Neither man spoke. There was nothing to say. Keith had murdered four people. He had done it to honor his brother. He had done it to rid the world of four people who preyed on children.

Mac sat, looked at the wall of the cell, smelled the scent of past and present bodies. He read the graffiti that would be scrubbed off later in the week. There were fresh messages, drawings.

"I Did Not Do This Crime This Time.—Big Ron."

"Not Fare. Just Not Fare.—Ollie from St. Paul."

"Warren Was Here."

Mac had been there for almost half an hour looking at the wall, hearing people in other cells cough and talk to themselves, listening to Keith Yunkin breathe. Mac sat patiently, preoccupied with his own thoughts of the past. He had time.

Then Keith spoke.

"Did the rain stop?"

"It stopped three days ago," said Mac.

"Who stopped the rain?"

Mac had no answer.

CSI: Miami

PC GAME
AVAILABLE NOW

Featuring the likenesses
of the entire CSI Miami cast

 CBS Consumer Products
 CBS PRODUCTIONS
 ALLIANCE ATLANTIS
 JERRY BRUCKHEIMER TELEVISION

THE DNA OF GREAT DVD

CSI: DVD 3